W9-AQN-103

Saint Peter's University Library
Withdrawn

THIS FIRST NOVEL by a young Negro discloses a fresh and amazing talent. At twenty-five, his feet dusty from wandering, William Attaway has brought to his publishers a book as poised, as perceptive, as honest and tender as many an older writer with a solid list of books behind him would be proud to claim. This is the story of Step and Ed, young men with no childhood behind them, no security before them; too young as yet to know complete despair, but old in the ways of hard, precarious living. Most of all it is the story of Hi Boy, a little Mexican boy of ten, who brought to Step and Ed a glimpse of unguessed integrities, who gave meaning to their lives. LET ME BREATHE THUNDER is that rare thing, a novel by a Negro about whites; a novel that reveals a powerful and objective talent at work upon the very fabric of life.

LET ME BREATHE THUNDER

WILLIAM ATTAWAY

LET ME
BREATHE THUNDER

THE CHATHAM BOOKSELLER
CHATHAM, NEW JERSEY

COPYRIGHT, 1939
BY DOUBLEDAY, DORAN & COMPANY, INC.
ALL RIGHTS RESERVED
CL

Reissued, 1969, by The Chatham Bookseller
by arrangement with Doubleday & Co., Inc.

Library of Congress Catalog Card No.: 70-96382

Printed in the United States of America

LET ME BREATHE THUNDER

WE WERE SEATED in the doorway of a boxcar, legs dangling. The ground was speeding away beneath our bare feet and the fields swung in a semicircle around the doorway of our "hobo pullman." The little Mexican boy who was between Step and me yelled gaily at a cow tethered in a field:

"Hi boy, hi boy, hi boy, hi . . ." And the cow was gone.

Step looked at me and laughed. The kid's high treble and singing tones always tickled him. I laughed with him just for the fun of it.

"Hi boy, hi," the little lad sang as we left a town behind.

"Ought to be in Seattle pretty soon," yelled Step, throwing his voice through cupped hands.

Boyish and full of friendliness for all things sounded the kid's cry again; we had just passed a farmer who had waved at us from his fields. Step reached over in mock anger and took the lad by the throat.

"Don't you know any other words?" And his grip became a rough caress.

The kid didn't know much more than his one greeting for the whole world: "Hi boy." We had just picked him up in New Mexico a week or so before, and all we had been able to get out of him was a few sentences:

"Family over there. . . . *Están allá, pero no*

encontrarlos. . . . Los molestaría mucho . . . yo,"
he had said and pointed when asked about his folks.
But this left us even more confused, for the pointing finger wavered this way and that until his people
might have been in any three or four places in the
Southwest at the same time.

"Sure, you're too young to be on the road," I had
chimed in. He could not have been more than nine
years old.

"Mucha trouble . . . run away *¡pronto!* Got ten
dollars," he said.

"Ed, you know some Mex. What's it all about?"
Step had appealed to me, but all my Spanish was on
the listening end. I couldn't ask him any questions.
What little I knew came from hearing the Spicks
jabber around on the quays. The kid had not lied
about the money, though. Step had it in his pocket
now for safekeeping.

"Am on road now?" the lad had asked after passing the money to Step.

3

"And how," was Step's answer, and he winked at me. We wanted to run out on him right away, but he was such a trusting little feller that we didn't have the heart. It was finally decided that he should go on to Seattle with us for a hot time.

It was a long trip but we always had more time on our hands than anything else, and distance doesn't mean a thing to a guy on the road. So because Seattle was a wide-open town, like it was just across the street instead of over a thousand miles away, we set out.

Step and me had been on the way to our regular summer round of the flat farm country before the kid came along, but the ten dollars changed our minds. We were just wandering handymen who never thought of work as long as there was a dollar to throw away in some city.

It was late afternoon when our freight pulled into the Seattle yards. The boy was asleep underneath Step's coat, for the day had turned cool. Step slapped at his shoes with the dog's tail he always carried and glanced enviously at my leather jacket.

"That tail's a hell of a thing to carry around."

"Almost in the home stretch," he said. "Time to wake up the kid."

"Whyn't you throw that thing away and get you a whole dog?"

"Butch wasn't just a dog."

"If that flyer had left the behind onto the tail, I suppose you'd carry that around too."

"He was mine, even if he was too dumb to dodge."

"He was my dog too, but that tail needs sun for awhile."

"This tail's luck," he said. "Luck and a smooth ride."

"Aw stuff, get the kid up," I told him. The train was slowly coming to a stop.

He shook the boy roughly and took the coat. Rubbing his eyes, the boy sat up.

"Put your shoes on. Time to bail out."

Through half-opened eyes the little lad looked into Step's face.

"Hi boy," he whispered sleepily.

Step felt my eyes on him.

"Time to get the hell out of here," he said, and pushed the boy out through the car door.

The three of us crouched by the side of a switch engine, anxiously scanning the yards for road detectives.

"No snakes around."

We struck out across the tracks. Before us were the hazy lights of the town, clean and beautiful now; soon to show the dirty streets of the waterfronts.

"Let's go to Hamburger Joe's first."

"Okay," agreed Step.

Passing through a square at the skirts of the city, we were stopped by the sight of a little fountain.

"Race you." And we were off.

I was the first to reach the water, and after a quick

6

drink I stepped back and began to tear off my clothes.

"Squirt the water on me . . . Squirt the water."

Step reached for the nozzle of the fountain, then he stopped.

"I say squirt the water," I cried. But there was something the matter with Step. The kid, too, had a strange look on his face. Suddenly I knew what the trouble was.

"Eee-ya, ee-ya!" we yelled, and did a war dance.

The lice were eating us up.

Throwing clothes right and left, half-hysterical with laughter, we swabbed each other down with water.

It was black night before we resumed our march on the city.

"Women or whisky? Women or whisky?" puzzled Step to himself.

"A beefsteak with mushrooms and onions," I exulted.

7

"Smokes, cigars," said the kid gravely. He pulled hard on an imaginary cigar.

"Okay, kid," cried Step, "we'll all smoke cigars . . . big black cigars."

On the way to Hamburger Joe's we had to pass through the red-light district and Step wanted to stop in one of the underground dives for a drink.

"Aw, c'mon, let's eat first," I begged. But he had to have his drink, so we went down the steps to a little basement saloon. We were stopped at the door.

"Can't bring that kid in here," snarled the bouncer.

"Okay, okay," said Step, drawing up his chest, "you don't have to get tough about it."

We took the kid back to the sidewalk and placed him on the curbing.

"Stay right here, now," commanded Step. "We'll be right out."

"Hi, hi, hi, hi boy." The kid was calling to the passing automobiles.

I felt kind of funny leaving him there all by himself, but I didn't want my buddy to think I was soft. I said nothing.

"A pony and two glasses," ordered Step, slapping the bar with the fat of his hand.

The whisky passed over the bar and we tried to toss it off without making faces. One round followed another. The hot coal in the pit of my stomach began to expand. I forgot about food. My image in the mirror across the bar grimaced foolishly at me. I grimaced foolishly back at it.

Step had drunk more than I had. His eyes were like quick snakes in his head. There was a woman seated at a table by the bar. His hot eyes settled on her and he walked the length of the bar to where she sat.

"Hello, sugar," he said thickly.

Evidently she didn't know much English, for she let out a stream of heavy Spanish phrases.

"Damn," said Step disgustedly, "a Spick."

"Sure, baby," said the woman.

"Okay, okay," said Step, grabbing her by the arm. "Have a drink."

He ordered more whisky.

"Speak English? English?" Step asked.

"Sure, baby," said the woman.

"Talk to her, Ed," he told me.

"Aw, c'mon, Step," I pleaded, "the kid's waiting."

"What the hell's eating you?" he snapped. "You know well as me we got to ditch that kid."

I just looked at him.

"Jeez, he can't go around with us," he said. "They won't let him in a bar, and we can't take him in any of them places."

There was logic in what he was saying, but it still didn't seem right . . . it being the kid's money and all.

"We'll give him back a couple of dollars," said Step. "An' I call that being damn soft."

I didn't say anything else. Step was a bad person to cross when he was drinking. He had done a turn in the ring, too, and whisky always made him quick with his fists.

"Suppose we take this Spick broad with us. Save picking up a dame later."

"Naw, we can go to a house," I said. I was still hoping that he would think of the kid after he sobered up.

"One dame is the same as another." He patted the woman's broad hips. "Jeez, here's woman enough for both of us."

"Okay," I gave in. "But you're the guy that 'll have to get rid of the kid."

Gathering up the change from the ten dollars, he led the way to the door. With no urging the woman followed. Just before we reached the steps the bouncer stopped us.

"You goddam tramp," he told the woman, "we told you before we don't allow no pickups in here."

"Sure, baby," said the woman.

"Now hold it a minute," began Step.

"You damn Spicks don't know a word of English when you get in a jam," said the man. "I'm wise to that stuff."

"I said hold it," repeated Step.

"That's all right, buddy," said the bouncer. "I ain't blaming you none. But she's been warned before in Spanish. She knows what I'm talking about."

"Sure, baby," said the woman.

"Just don't give a damn if we get closed up, do you?"

He hit her across the breast with the side of his hand. She fell back against the door, all her pain held, like a bitch dog, in her eyes.

"Sure, baby," she whimpered.

I tried to grab Step's arm but I was not quick enough. His clenched fist raked the bouncer's chin, and with the follow-through his elbow stabbed at the dazed man's eyes. A knee in the pit of the stomach left just a helpless dummy for the quick fist and elbow to cut to pieces. Step was like a madman. He did not try to knock the man down. It satisfied him to turn the bouncer's face into a mass of long red welts.

"Lay off, Step. Lay off," I yelled, but I could not hold him. The face began to turn into just a piece of pulpy meat.

The bartender sprinted around the bar and tried to help me save the bouncer. Step turned and struck savagely at us.

"Don't let him kill him," cried the bartender. "They'll close my place up if he kills him."

I picked up a beer bottle. There was nothing left to do. I couldn't let him kill a man. He had had to quit the ring because he went mad like this when he started hitting a man.

The bottle was aimed for the side of Step's head, but he moved and it caught him on the cheekbone. He went down like the cattle used to fall when I had that job polling steers at the St Louis stockyards. The bouncer was still on his feet. He would have fallen across Step if the bartender had not held him up.

"Get him out of here," said the bartender. "Better get him out of town too. This guy has a lot of friends. They won't like this."

I threw the dregs of some beer in Step's face and in a few minutes he opened his eyes. Because he looked up at me and smiled, I knew he was dead sober.

"You didn't have to hit me so hard," he said.

I helped him to his feet.

"The bottle slipped," I told him.

He still would not go without the woman. She had been crouched behind the door during the fight. It was easy to see that she was scared to death of him, but she went with us to the sidewalk. The Mexican boy was still seated on the curbing where we had left him.

"Hi, hi," he sang when he saw us.

We stood looking at him. The woman stood with

us. Her eyes were dull lead in her face. She was an animal waiting for her master's mind that would be her mind.

"Okay, you tell him," I said to Step.

The kid sat with his eyes on us, unsurprised at sight of the woman. He was, probably, not the kind of kid to be surprised at anything. His attention finally wandered to the street again and his lips moved in a soundless "Hi boy, hi."

"Go ahead, tell him."

Step rubbed his face where the beer bottle had left a great purple splotch. His brow knitted in heavy thought.

"Didn't have to hit me so hard," he muttered absent-mindedly. He glanced quickly at the woman.

"Sure, baby," jerked from her lips.

"Look here, Sure Baby," he said. "I changed my mind. Go peddle your papers."

She looked, uncomprehending.

"I mean for you to scram . . . blow." He gave

15

her a little shove. She got the idea and backed away a few steps. Then she stopped.

"Here, wait a minute," he said, and pushed a couple of bills into her hand. She was holding the money limply as we went away. I guess she never met anybody like Step before.

We did not go to Hamburger Joe's. We walked around the city. Step bought some frankfurters and a bag of rolls, and we walked along munching and saying nothing. Even the kid was silent. I was surprised when Step remembered to buy the cigars.

Late that morning we found a city park and settled down at the edge of a duck pond to wait for dawn. The kid fell asleep. Step took the lighted cigar out of the little feller's hand, snuffed it out and put it away. His jaw was paining him and he did not feel like smoking. The grayness that came at four-thirty found us there watching the ducks that kept up a riotous "ha . . . ha . . . ha . . ." and

16

thinking that life was not so simple as it had been before we met Hi Boy.

"Get on your coat, we got to get going." That was how quick we left Seattle. It wasn't because Step was afraid of what the bouncer's friends might do, it was simply that a transient cannot afford to get into trouble. He insisted on us riding the cushions as long as we had money.

"You got to remember," he told me when I protested, "we ain't real hoboes. We're out looking for a job of work."

"But where we going?"

"Far as these tickets on the N.P. will take us, stupid."

"That ain't very far."

"All right, then, we'll jump a freight after that. There's a farm around the Snake River. Be plowing for wheat now . . . need good men."

I didn't say anything more. I was just as eager as
he to see how it felt to be a millionaire. Riding on
the inside did not excite the kid, however; he
seemed to take everything for granted. Almost as
soon as we boarded the passenger he slumped back
on his neck and let his eyelids droop.

"Where you fellers headed?" the conductor who
punched the tickets asked. Smiling, he plumped
down on the arm of Step's seat. I could see he was
just a guy who was lonesome. A lot of people don't
do any more than pass the time of day with a conductor.

"Don't the tickets say?" asked Step.

"That ain't hardly a water stop," said the conductor. "Ain't nothing there but Spick and Mex
shacks."

"Well, that's where we're going," said Step.

"You fellers don't look like foreigners."

Step pulled up the kid's head by the thick oily
hair.

18

"See this kid?"

The conductor looked into the boy's face.

"Hi boy," said the kid gravely.

"Yeah, he's Mex all right," admitted the conductor.

"Well, I'm the kid's paw."

"I'll be jiggered."

Step was looking so levelly into the man's eyes that I could almost have swallowed the story myself.

"Some bruise you got there," said the conductor, noticing Step's discolored face. "Accident, maybe?"

"Naw, that was tattooed on," said Step. "Used to be a mermaid but I washed my face and the colors run."

The conductor started to smile but Step kept a straight face.

"What was you doing in Seattle?" asked the conductor after a pause. He should have had sense enough by that time to let Step alone.

"The kid was in school there," was the answer, "but we had to take him out. He learned so much they was scared to learn him any more until his head grew bigger."

The conductor looked like he wanted to laugh or apologize for something, I don't know which. Step didn't give him a chance to make up his mind. He pointed to me.

"That there's the kid's maw, we . . ."

There wasn't need to finish that lie. The conductor turned as red as skinned beef and started off down the aisle. Step gave a cruel little laugh.

"Aw, what 'd you do that for?" I asked.

"Nuts to you," he growled back.

"The poor guy was just lonesome," I said. "How'd you like to be riding a train all the time without nobody to talk to?"

"Stop, you're killing me," he mocked.

"Then if you got somebody to talk to, there wouldn't be nothing to talk about 'cause people don't talk about nothing important to conductors."

20

Step got serious.

"Jeez, there's other guys on this train, why'd he have to pick on us?"

"Maybe we look like good guys," I said.

"The hell we do. We look like guys what ain't used to riding the cushions. Maybe we look like bums on the stem, or something. Maybe we look like guys what don't amount to nothing, so he figgers he can get familiar with us."

"We don't amount to nothing," I told him.

"I notice he ain't taking off his cap and flopping down in the seat with that guy what's got the iron hat on." He pointed at a fat-faced man in a stiff collar and derby hat.

"He don't look like such a good guy from the back," I said.

"Well, we bought our tickets just like he did," argued Step. "We got a right just like him not to have the conductor get too familiar. We ain't on the outside now, we're on the cushions."

"A hell of a difference that makes."

"It makes a lot of difference," said Step. "For all that conductor knows our fathers might own a ten-thousand-acre sheep ranch. We might be dressed like this because we been out herding just for the fun of it."

"Aw, what's the use of making up something about us that ain't so?"

We might have kept bickering back and forth like that and forgotten to enjoy the ride if the kid hadn't come to life.

"Water . . . want water."

"Show him how to get some water," said Step.

"Show him yourself," I told him. I was still peeved enough to dislike the way he had kind of ordered me to do it.

"All right," he said, "go on and be a jackass."

When he took the kid by the hand and led him down the aisle I forgot my peeve. It was funny to see him give the man in the iron hat a hard stare as he

22

and the kid went by—kinda like he was daring the man to think anything. By the time they got back I was grinning all over myself. Step began to grin too. He and the kid sat down. We kept grinning.

"Jeez, but you look like a fool," he said. And we both laughed.

The conductor came through the car and the kid, excited by our good humor, yelled after him:

"Hi boy, hi boy, hi boy."

The conductor did not look around. His back was very businesslike. By the look on Step's face I knew that he was ashamed of something.

The dining-car waiter came through in the conductor's wake.

"Last call for lunch . . . Last call for lunch . . . Last call for lunch . . . Last call . . ." And he was out the other end of the car. The memory of him made me hungry: brown skin and spotless white suit.

The man in the iron hat got up and went forward. Step, who had made several efforts to express what he was sorry about, watched the man in the iron hat go forward.

"You game to eat in the diner?" burst out of him. He hadn't meant to say that.

"Hungry enough to eat," said the kid, rubbing his stomach.

Step pushed the point when he saw me hesitate.

"I still got six bits left," he said. "Ought to be able to get enough for the three of us on that."

I looked at his wrinkled coat.

"Aw, we ain't dressed right."

"We got our tickets," he said. "What's the matter, getting yellow?"

"You know that ain't so. It's just that you can tell we sleep in our clothes."

"Me and Hi Boy's going in the diner," he stated. "Coming or not?"

Looking back over his shoulder at me, he herded the kid into the aisle. I followed. The kid didn't

24

know what it was all about, but Step and me kept hunching our shoulders and fumbling with the buttons on our coats as we walked.

There were only three or four people in the diner —that made us feel better. I wanted to slide into one of the chairs at the very end table but for some reason we had to walk hard on our heels to the center of the car. Everybody looked around at us and we tried to act like it was a joke that we were so dirty.

"Eat boy, eat boy, eat boy," sang the kid happily.

"The kid's a laugh, ain't he?" said Step loudly. But Step wasn't tickled—he looked miserable.

Everything was so white. The people looked whiter than any I had ever seen before. Once I was in a restaurant in Detroit and a very black boy had come in walking hard on his heels. Everybody had looked at him. Now I glanced down at my hands to see if they hadn't turned dark. The waiter hadn't served the black boy.

The waiter did not come for a long time.

"These mountains sure are swell mountains," said Step, looking out of the window. He was still talking too loud.

"Yeah, sure are swell," I said. "Look, Hi Boy . . . look at the mountains."

"Sure, swell swell mountains," mimicked the kid.

"Any mountains where you come from, kid?" asked Step.

"Everybody knows they got mountains in Mexico," I said. "They got mountains everywhere."

"How come you got to talk so loud?" whispered Step.

"I ain't talking loud, it's you," I whispered back.

"Well, let the kid answer." He was shouting again. "Hi Boy ain't no dummy."

"What you getting on me for?"

"I ain't getting on you." He glanced around defiantly.

The train was circling the rim of a gorge. There was a straight drop to the tops of the pines five or six hundred feet below. The sunlight hit the scrubs on the slope above us and filtered down into the gorge, piercing it with great jagged shadows. Behind the far rim of the great cut that was like a part in the hair of the piny mountains lay tier after tier of ranges; each successive range more cloudlike than the one before, until the very last line of rolling gray became the rind of the sky.

We forgot the diner.

"Maybe they got mountains in Mexico, maybe not," said Step absent-mindedly.

The kid gazed away in the distance. His eyes were soft and mystical looking. He was far away at some place that must have been so simple and beautiful that only a child's mind could bear to go there. His eyes rose with a mountain whose peak was lost in white and mist.

"*Vivo muy arriba, allá,*" he stated simply.

There was a moment of great quiet. We both were looking wistfully at him, as if we wanted to ask him not to go there again without taking us with him.

"Too bad that people have to grow up and come down off the mountains," said a deep voice from across the aisle.

We whirled. It was the fat-faced man in the iron hat. Only he didn't have the hat on now. We didn't know what to say to him.

"Yeah," said Step noncommittally, turning away.

I could see that he resented the man catching us off guard. I hadn't liked it at the moment, but when the stranger smiled and turned back to his meal I could see that he hadn't meant to butt in on us. Most likely he had felt in the kid the same things we had. And now that the iron hat was up on a hook, I could see that he wasn't such a bad-looking guy. His face was reddened and crinkled, with eyes squinched up like they were looking into the sun. Wind and shine must have been in his face for many

a long morning before breakfast. The face of a
rancher, but I had never seen a rancher who wore
city clothes that looked like they might have been
made for him.

"What 'll it be, sirs?" It was the waiter standing
over our table.

Step thought for a moment.

"Well, what you got?"

The waiter picked the menu from behind the
salt and pepper shakers and gave it to him. Step
flushed.

"I might suggest that you would like the luncheonette," said the waiter, before Step's fumbling
hands could open the folded card. Annoyed, my
buddy looked up at the brown face. The waiter saw
the blood-purpled bruise and his eyes widened.

"Okay, okay, bring what you said."

Step looked ominously after the retreating white
coat.

"The next sonofabitch who asks me about my

29

face is going to find out how it happened damn sudden," he gritted.

"But he ain't asked you nothing."

"Well, he wanted to ask. Everybody in this car wants to ask."

I didn't say anything more about that because, after all, it was me who hit him with the bottle and made the bruise. He might still have gotten sore at me if that had crossed his mind.

"How much do they charge for food here?" I asked it just to change the subject. I was sure we had enough money.

"Can't be more than six bits," said Step. "He didn't say dinner or supper; he didn't even say lunch—he said luncheonette."

"Yeah, and, too, we didn't order no sides or nothing."

"Just straight luncheonette," he grinned, putting his hands on his hips and switching about in the chair like a sissy.

30

"Straight luncheonette, just straight," followed the kid, putting his hands on his hips and trying to act like Step.

We were still laughing at him when the waiter brought the food, and that was quite awhile.

"Double lamb chops, charcoal grilled." The waiter stood there smiling like he was glad for us to have gotten such good food.

With a little cry of pleasure the kid grabbed up his chop in his fists and started to tear into the meat. Quick as a flash, Step rapped him over the knuckles.

"What do you think they got knives and forks on here for?"

Blankly, the kid looked at him.

"Watch me," he commanded, and he picked up a knife and tried to cut the meat. The chop kept sliding around the plate, so he held it down with one hand while he cut off a piece. "So," he breathed smugly, as he speared it with his fork and carried it to his mouth.

I watched Step in amazement. I didn't know much about him, except that at the country fairs he used to fight all comers to make a living. He had never talked about his home. This insistence on some kind of table manners made me curious about his past. He had not gone to high school as I had, I knew that. And where, other than school, could fellers like us pick up table manners?

The waiter tried to help the kid who was making a mess of his food in trying to imitate Step.

"This kid's my son," said Step. "I got to learn him something." That was the second time he had told the same lie, but now he said it like he, himself, believed it.

"Oh." The waiter tried to back away.

"Trot back and draw three, boy," ordered Step.

"What's that?" puzzled the waiter.

"Java . . . Java . . . three cups."

The kid just could not learn to use the knife, so Step finally reached over and used it for him. That left his fingers greasy, so he wiped them carefully on the napkin and then tucked the smeared cloth in his collar. With such an example, I did not dare to pick up my meat. I followed suit and went at it the hard way—with a knife.

After coffee came the check. The waiter laid it face downward and went away quickly. Step picked it up. The satisfied look left his face.

"Sonofabitch."

"What's the matter?"

"No wonder the darky turned that check down and beat it," he said, and pushed the blue square of paper toward me.

I stared with amazement at the figures.

"Two dollars and fifty-five cents, and sixty cents for coffee." It was unbelievable.

"There's some mistake." He beckoned the waiter.

"That ain't our bill," I said.

The waiter had not made any mistake. He showed us the menu. We gazed at it for a long time.

33

"Okay," said Step. "We just wanted to make sure."

"What we going to do?" I whispered after the waiter had gone.

"Don't know yet," he said. Reaching in his pocket he took out the six bits, counting the money and matching it against the check. Suddenly he grabbed the dozing kid by the shoulder and shook him awake. "Look, kid," he ordered, "go on through the train to the last platform. When the train stops drop down to the tracks and crawl like hell."

"What about us?" I whispered.

"We'll make a run for it."

Both Step and I were trembling as the kid got up, but the little feller did not seem a bit scared.

"Now don't forget to crawl like hell."

"Okay." He strolled back through the train.

We sat for awhile, then Step reached in his pocket and got out the cigar butt he had been saving for the kid.

"Got to be doing something until this train stops," he explained as he lit the stub.

"When will that be?"

"No telling. We'll have to puff easy on this roach."

"Are we getting out the same way as the kid?"

"We'll have to open a door. It's quicker. It'll go off all right if we don't have to be bothered with the half-pint."

"Yeah."

For years we sat trying to make conversation, then at last there was nothing more to say. So we just passed the cigar butt back and forth between us and wished like hell that the train would stop. The butt was burning our fingers before we finally began to slow down.

"Get ready, she's blowing for a town."

I was ready.

Faint and far away came the whistle again, and suddenly houses began to flash by. There was a clanging of bells as we passed a crossing. A girl in one of the automobiles waiting on the highway waved frantically at everyone she saw on the train. We waved back at her, and from the rear platform we could hear the kid's "Hi boy, hi." With the train barely moving we tensed ourselves for the run. We were waiting for that jangle that would mean the engineer was giving the air brakes all the pressure they could stand.

"Everything all right, sirs?" It was the dining-car waiter standing in front of our table.

"Damn," I breathed.

"Everything's okay," said Step tensely.

"More coffee?" suggested the waiter.

"Naw . . ."

He picked up the check, put it on a little tray and extended it suggestively toward Step. We heard the jangle we were waiting for.

"Guess I'll just have to let this guy have it," whispered Step.

He got up and pushed his chair back. I set myself

36

to hop over the waiter, for it was sure that in a moment he would be on the floor. Step's left arm came back.

"Just a minute there." A voice.

We held ourselves.

"I'll take those boys' check," said the voice across the aisle.

The waiter looked relieved. He gave the man our check, got his money and left. The man looked across to us.

"Better call back your little friend," he said.

I ran through the cars to the back platform and there was Hi Boy sitting on the railing, hands in his pockets. I hauled him back.

"You little fool. Whyn't you wait till the train stopped?"

"I ready jump . . . crawl like hell."

"Yeah, and if the train had hit a curve your juice would have dripped all over the tracks."

Back in the coach the man in the derby was waiting. He sat in the seat facing Step and me, his arm around Hi Boy's shoulders. For one of the few times since I had known him Step showed great dignity:

"That was a swell thing to do. Maybe we'll be able to stand up for you sometime," he said.

"Forget it," the man told him.

"You know how it is when you lose your pocket-book," said Step.

Inwardly, I groaned. So Step was not going to play straight after all. I had hoped that we were going to be able to be just ourselves. And Step had started lying already.

"Sure . . . sure . . . I used to lose my pocket-book a lot, too, when I was your age."

Step looked suspicious, but the full crinkled face did not suggest double talk.

"Yeah, yeah," he said.

"You see," the man went on, "I kinda had an idea that I owed you fellers the price of a meal anyway."

"How's that?" Step and me spoke together.

38

"It's sorta hard to explain, but I'll try." He rubbed the kid's head where it dozed in the circle of his arm.

"Crawl like hell," whispered the kid.

"Suppose your mind was tangled up in a lot of little things—future of apples on the market, trees to be pruned, truck to be put in the ground, orchard ground to be broken for auxiliary crops, lambs to be castrated, desert irrigation, pheasants shot out of season on your ranch, a nest of rattlesnakes under your back doorstep . . ."

"That's tough," sighed Step.

"Yeah," I agreed.

"Oh, it isn't so tough," laughed the man, as he looked at our serious faces. "Especially when some fellers happen along who show you that there are some bigger things to think about. Mountaintops, for instance." He rubbed the kid's head again.

I liked the way the man talked, but there was a half-sneer on Step's face. Maybe he didn't like to be reminded how the man had caught us with our guard down back in the diner.

"Suppose you fellers tell me something about yourselves," said the man.

Neither one of us spoke.

"That is, if you feel like it," he added.

"Sure, sure, we don't mind," said Step. "Course my brother and me hates to air our troubles . . ."

It was out. The sneer had meant that Step took the man for one of those sentimental suckers. We were always meeting up with people, mostly females, who wanted to make pitiful figures of us—and were mostly willing to pay for the sad, sad tale of our lives. Poor little boys of the road, they called us. We never disappointed them. That "brother" gag was one of the first things we always pulled on them. I could have told the rest of Step's tale backwards in pig Latin.

"I can appreciate that feeling," the man was saying.

40

"We ain't really bums or nothing," said Step. "We're fellers out looking for a job of work to send our mother to a sanatorium. She broke herself down washing clothes to put us boys through school."

"And your father was a drunkard, I suppose," said the man.

"Naw, the old man was a sailor. Was drowned in a hurricane off the Cape of Good Hope. Might have saved hisself, too, if he'd been of a mind—he could swim like a fish—but he stayed by the captain and went down with the ship. That's what captains are s'posed to do, you know."

"So I've read in storybooks."

Step gave him the suspicious eye but continued:

"So there we was. Left with no money and nobody to turn to. The old lady took in washing to keep us boys in school. So, Jeez, by the time we got to going good she was ready for a wheelchair. I was set to be a lawyer. My brother, here, was going to go in for doctor work. But we talked it over and decided to give all that up and go out in the world to find us a job of work and send the old lady up for the rest cure . . ."

Step paused like he was expecting a little praise, but the man sat and touched his finger tips together.

"So far," said Step, "we ain't found no kind of work that lasted long; but everything we make, or anybody gives us, we send home to Ma."

The man did not reach in his pocketbook like he was supposed to.

"Haven't you forgotten something?" he asked my buddy.

That kind of shocked Step.

"What's that!"

"About the kid here."

"Oh, him—he's a neighbor's kid. An orphan . . . That is, his folks died," stuttered Step.

"I understand."

That was the end of that, and we just leaned back

42

and watched the country roll by. After a long while the man turned back to us.

"You boys know anything about sheep?"

"I do," said Step.

"Might have a little work for you out my place, Four Mile Farm, in the Yakima Valley. Of course the pay ain't much—just eight dollars a month apiece."

"It ain't much as we're used to getting," said Step, "but it ain't hay." By the grin on his face I knew just what he was thinking.

"Well, if you decide to come you can't miss the place. Like the name says, just four miles outside the town."

"You ain't told us your name," I said.

"Sampson. Everybody in Yakima knows Sampson."

"My pardner's name is Step; mine is Ed," I told him. "Oh, and we just call the kid, there, Hi Boy."

Sampson shook our hands like we had just met. He pulled out a cigar and bit off the end.

43

"Excuse me," he said, reaching back in his coat, "do you boys smoke cigars?"

Something in the way he asked the question made me want to deny that we smoked.

"No, we don't," I blurted before Step had a chance to open his mouth.

"That's funny, would have sworn I saw you smoking back in the diner," smiled Sampson.

Step gave me a long hard look. I could hardly stand the pressure of his eyes. Squirming about, I grew as little as possible in my seat.

It was late afternoon when the conductor came through and curtly announced:

"You fellers get off next stop."

"Maybe I'd better write down the name of the farm and all," said Sampson, "so's you won't forget." On the back of a card he scribbled something with a silver pencil. "Now there'll be no excuse, unless you just don't like work." He gave the card to Step.

Sampson waved at us as we stood by the roadbed

watching them haul down the spout of the water tower. We waved back, and the kid sang out his "Hi boy" as the engineer gave the whistle two sharp toots.

"There's the highball," remarked Step.

The train gathered momentum and in a couple of minutes was gone.

"After that, I suppose you won't be satisfied with freights any more," I said to Step.

"Oh, I don't know," he said. And laughing with all his old freedom, he cried: "C'mon, you fellers, there's a water hydrant. . . . Race you."

We wandered in and out among the Mex and Spick shacks. Most of the men were away working on a roadbed five or six miles down the right-of-way, an old woman told us. From her we got corn-cakes and all the goat's milk we could drink for a dime. She kept looking at the kid.

45

"Where that feller's folks?" she finally asked.

"C'mon, let's go," said Step quickly.

We walked back to the tracks. The kid wandered over to a grassy strip and began to run and kick at the clover and puffballs.

"Six-week lambs act just like that," remarked Step.

"What about that card?" I asked. "Are we going to Sampson's 'stead of the wheat lands?"

"Naw, I was just stringing him. It's the big thousand-acre farms for us."

I had hoped that we would be trailing Sampson but I didn't say anything. I had followed Step for years. He said the wheat lands, so that was where we would be going. He took the card out of his pocket and held it between two fingers.

"Might as well get rid of this. I hate to work around sheep, anyway."

"A thousand acres is a lot of hard ground."

"You don't know sheep."

He had been turning the card in his fingers and the writing on the back caught his eye.

"Well, I'm a sonofabitch."

The kid came running.

"What is it?" I asked.

"If this don't beat all hell," said Step. "The guy writes his name and everything but, Jeez, underneath he says: 'I don't believe that poor liars are always poor workers.'"

"What you think he meant by that?"

"Aw, the guy was hep to us all the time," said Step. "He wasn't swallering that story a little bit."

"Did you ever get fooled?" I howled.

The kid howled too. I don't think he knew why.

"Yessir, he had his hip boots, all right," said Step with grudging admiration.

To my mind, that settled it. He would never go to the Yakima Valley now. Laughing, I watched him pull the lucky dog tail out of his pocket, throw it in the air and mark the direction in which it pointed.

47

"Cut the 'hee haw,' and let's find somebody who knows when a freight pulls through here," he said briskly.

"What's the hurry all of a sudden?"

He slapped the tail against his thigh.

"Tail says to follow Sampson, and by God we'll do it. We'll go to the Yakima Valley."

Sheets of invisible rain came in the night. The three of us crouched under a sheet of corrugated tin propped against the water tower. The "slow drag" that we were going to hitch onto was down a half mile on a siding to let a fast passenger ball through on the right-of-way. The kid was covered with my leather jacket but the jacket had been soaked through when I gave it to him. It must have made him wetter and more miserable because his whimpers could be heard through the roar of water as it drummed against the corrugated tin.

48

Step and me had been through other nights like this one. We were cold as hell too, but knew how to joke and keep up our spirits.

"Oughtn't be a cloud left nowheres, after this," said Step.

I threw a rock into the black. There was a splash.

"Must be the ocean out there."

Step threw a rock and listened for the splash.

"C'mon, Hi Boy," he called, "c'mon, throw some rocks and help fill up the ocean."

The kid did not move toward us.

"Aw, you cry baby," Step said.

He leaned over me to pull at the kid.

"C'mon, kid, laugh."

I could feel Step's arm jerk as the kid squirmed away.

"I cold, cold, *mis manos son heladas,*" he kept repeating.

Step got tired of it.

"Ain't going to help none to cry," he said. "Don't

you think we're cold? Feel Ed, here." He pulled the kid's hand over to my wet chest. "He's in his shirt sleeves, but do you think he'd holler?"

The kid's hand was trembling, and it sounded as though his mouth made little noises in spite of himself.

"Aw, goddam you, you're yellow," grunted Step. "We can't have no yellowbellies traveling with us."

"Give him a break, he ain't nothing but a kid," I said.

"Jeez, he's old enough to show yellow," said Step. Without seeing, I could feel him turn his back on the kid. To emphasize his complete withdrawal he started up a new conversation: "You should of re- minded me to get a sack o' tobacco. A guy oughtn't to be without a smoke on a night like this." The very tone excluded Hi Boy from the wish-tobacco.

The kid moved up against me. His body was hot against my side. It would have been better for all of us to have snuggled together in a heap, but Step and me were funny about things like that. We were always so anxious to prove to each other how much we could stand. So he sat apart, and I was glad it was too dark for him to see me enjoying the heat of the kid's body.

Long before we heard the rattle of the speeding passenger, we saw the glare of the headlight and heard the trailing whistle that always means a train is balling along.

"Jeez, she's coming like a bat out of hell."

The piercing headlight was a wedge in the rainy night, holding it apart in two towering black walls. The engine screamed again, wildly; the slow freight answered with a short blast, and the broken lights of the coaches were flickering past. A brief glimpse of diners, sleepers, fat men smoking in a club car; then the red letters on the rear of the observation platform: Moonlight Flyer.

The night closed in again, and the train had been only a dream.

"C'mon, that slow drag will be pulling any minute." Step brought me back to the present.

Clambering up the cinder incline of the roadbed, we ran down the siding toward the lights that marked the freight. Step had ignored Hi Boy altogether. I dragged him along by one sleeve of the jacket. There wasn't any time to lose; they had taken on water already.

I was the first one to find the refrigerator car. Calling to Step, I ran the rungs to the top. If only the ice compartments were empty, we could get warm in a "reefer." Opening the trap, I peered down.

"Any ice?" called Step from the ground.

"C'mon up, no ice. Must be a lettuce car."

In a flash he and the kid were at my side. He fished in his pocket and brought out a dry match. He always did that. You never can tell what you'll find in a "reefer." A scratch and he was holding the flame down in it.

52

There were three men on the floor of the compartment.

"You ain't no snakes, are you, buddy?" came from the depths. The voice was whining, without confidence.

"Naw . . . Any room?" asked Step.

"There's three of us, but c'mon down. Be warmer with more."

Six fellers in a "reefer," clicking along in the night. We sat shoulder to shoulder, our damp clothes steaming. It was pleasant to be in out of the weather; it made me drowsy. The next thing I remember was waking with my head on Step's shoulder, the kid half across my lap. Someone had lit the stump of a candle and all eyes were strung to the flame. The air was thick with human steam and smoke. It all smelled good.

"You awake?" asked Step.

I sat up guiltily.

"Want a smoke?"

He passed me a sack of tobacco and a brown paper bag. Bag paper is good to roll your tobacco in when you are out of the regular tissue. I did not bother to thank anybody. It didn't matter whose tobacco it was. That was the way with fellers on the road: they always shared their smokes. With my cigarette lit, I tore off another piece of the bag and rolled one for Hi Boy. It took a lot of shaking to wake him up.

"Here, kid, smoke this."

I settled back, drawing clouds of warm smoke in my lungs, feeling that time had taken the night off . . . that we were away from anything real . . . like calm drifting in the still air; an air to make men tell things that they would regret when daylight came. Lazily, I glanced along my shoulder at the faces of the three strange men. One face was small and wizened, with little bald eyelids like pieces of lemon peel; one was concealed in whiskers, but the eyes were hunted and shifty; the third was black . . . moons flashing in a face merged with the shadows.

Those were the points of the faces I saw. I was in the mood to catch nothing but high lights; and between periods when I must have dozed, I caught the following high lights in their conversation:

"Been riding long?" Step asked the wizened-faced one.

"Five hours. Me and them too," he gestured.

"Where you headed?"

"Just eastways."

"Your buddies too?"

"Never saw them 'fore tonight."

"We're all headed just eastways, buddy," said Shifty Eyes, without seeming to move his lips.

"Where you fellers headed to?" asked the black one.

"Off at Yakima."

"Good place in August. I've knocked apples there."

"Yeah, might be good country to stop in when a feller gets too old to knock around," said Step.

"Reckon I'll pick the city when I cotton on one place for good," said Wizened Face.

"Me, I'll always be moving," said the shifty-eyed one. And as if he'd said too much: "Anyway, when the road gets you you'd sooner be moving."

"I reckon I thought I was going to stay put a hundred times," said the black face, "but somehow I always catch myself moving on."

"An' a good thing it is to move on. Dicks never forget, and if they should happen to forget they got it all written down somewhere in the White House." The man who did not seem to move his lips glanced about nervously as he spoke.

"Ain't hard to get on relief now," said Wizened Face, "but I never can seem to get settled on what city."

"No sense a-tall in a feller running round the country when there's steady jobs he can get," said

the black face. "Still, somehow, I always catch myself moving on."

"I ain't gonna knock around from job to job
till I get to be a million years old," said Step. "After
I seen the whole world and every kind of dame in
it, I'm gonna hold me down one job of work and
marry with somebody soft as a movie star."

This was a new Step. Of course I knew that one
day I would settle down, but Step——

"Well, I wouldn't never marry no dame," said
Shifty Eyes. "You sour on them and they run quick
an' tell everything on you they know."

"That's one thing about the city," leered Wizened
Face. "Jeez, what broads."

"When I settles down it's gonna be where I can
still mix with guys on the road," said Black Face.
"Guys on the road ain't got prejudice like other
folks."

"Them city broads . . ." dreamed Wizened Face.

"Why, I was coming into Chi from Wichita last

year or last month, or something," continued Black Face. "There was a yeller-haired girl in the empty with a bunch of us. Some of them gave her money. She let me love her up all the way in to Chi for a piece of cake."

"If I ever do come across a place safe to settle in, it won't be with no dame," declared Shifty Eyes.

"Yessir, all the way into Chi. Black or white, it's all the same on the road."

"You ever see 'em sitting in store windows in Seattle?" asked Wizened Face. "If you're cute enough about it you can flash a phony bill and they'll give you a tumble."

The black face swayed with the candle shadows. "I had a gal onct in Alabama. Man, but she could go. Guess I would've married up with her too, but I got to thinking 'bout raisin' colored kids in Alabama. Was gonna send for her when I found a better place, but jobs give out 'bout that time. I just kept moving."

"One dame ain't no more 'n another," said Step. "It's according how you look at it. They all was give the same thing by God."

"Before I got ruled off the track, when I was bringing 'em in under the wire, always in the money, I used to have as many as five dames in my room every night," said Wizened Face. "Them was the days."

"I was hitched once. The bitch ratted on me," snarled Shifty Eyes, choking the air between his claws.

"Jobs ain't so hard to get now. Maybe I might write that Alabama gal one of these days when I settles down."

"Been a long time . . . Might could get me a job at the tracks, somewhere they run horses, if I could stay put. Dames and horses again, I ain't too old for either one."

"The priest that tied the knot, even he told me she was no good. And now I never will be able to stop movin'. He was a smart man, that priest . . . he was a good man." The shifty eyes were motionless for a second.

"Preachers and ministers and such—ain't none of them worth a one-dollar bet on a two-legged horse," declared the ex-jockey.

The eyes in the black face flickered like paper lanterns in a strong wind.

"See that kid?" The ex-jockey pointed at Hi Boy. "He looks sort of like a girl. Ain't I right?" he asked.

"Cut it," warned Step, and his voice teetered on the edge of dangerous.

"That's all right, buddy, I ain't trying to horn in on nothing," cringed the man. He laughed evilly and glanced across at Hi Boy again. Step drew himself up, but he couldn't stop the guy from laughing suggestively under his breath.

It seemed like trouble might start. I listened for a moment to the wash of rain driven against the side of the car.

"Anybody here that's looking for trouble 'll see heaven damn soon," broke out Step. I felt his shoulders stiffen.

Nobody wanted to take up the challenge.

The man with the shifty eyes picked up the candle. A flurry of rain drummed against the trap door. He blew out the candle.

We could almost spit from the freight to the middle of sunlit Yakima. The girls here mostly wore pants, drove their father's trucks into town and took steps like men. Step got fresh with a couple of them who were fixing a flat tire near the tracks. They cursed him, using good round oaths. He walked on. The kid and me wanted to stand by the pens that faced the railroad tracks and watch the men load sheep into the latticelike cars, but we had to follow Step. After all, he had been here before and we didn't know the town. He should have been feeling good because the swelling on his face had gone down, but he wasn't. The lambs bawled, and the kid, who was himself again, trilled:

"Hi boy, hi boy, hi boy, hi."

The loaders turned and waved to him because the cry was bright and joyful as the sunlight.

"Shut up, it might rain some more," was Step's remark. He was still off Hi Boy.

For a minute I thought the kid was going to cry, he looked so miserable. But he didn't, and I reached out and took his hand.

"You know where you're going?" I asked Step after we had walked a distance.

"To see Mag. Friend of mine."

I had heard about Mag before. Step admired her a whole lot. It seemed that she had been just a two-bit whore until she had come to Yakima many years before. She had not gone the way most women like her go. She had saved her money and put it into real estate and houses. Now, at fifty-three years of age, she owned a sizable stretch of land facing the tracks, a roadhouse and several houses. She had something on the ball, Step had said.

Mag, herself, came to the door at our knock. She was fat and black as a tar ball. I was knocked off my feet for a second. Step had not told me she was black. As soon as she saw Step she gave a whoop and grabbed him around the shoulders.

"Well, roast me for a turkey," she cried. "What kind of white trash has the wind blowed in?"

"And are you looking good," laughed Step. "Why, nobody would think you was a day over two hundred."

She laughed with him and it was impossible to believe that she was almost twice old enough to be my mother.

"This is my buddy, Ed."

"Well, I'm right happy to meet up with you then, child." She looked at the kid. I could see that Step was not going to introduce him. It's funny how that guy can hold onto a grouch.

"That's Hi Boy," I told her.

"Say, but he's a little feller." She felt his ribs. "Looks like he could use some biscuits."

"I ain't any too fat around the backbone, myself," said Step.

"Well, what the hell you standing out here for?" she cried. "C'mon in and fall to."

In no time at all we were seated at a table, gulping down great mouthfuls of ham and eggs. She hadn't been fooling about the biscuits, either. They were big and flaky.

"This ain't near appletime. You fellers must be just stopping through," said Mag.

"Naw, going out to a guy's farm to fool with sheep."

"Not many sheep right around here. Must be Sampson's."

"Yeah, that's it."

"Must have seen them loading some of his lambs down at the pens, didn't you?" asked Mag.

"Guess we did," said Step. "Say, what kind of an egg is he, anyway?"

"Damn good feller. Been here in this valley twenty-odd year."

"Reckon you know near everybody in and out of Yakima since the town was a town, don't you?" I asked.

"Ain't trying to find out how old I am, are you, young feller?"

"Oh no . . . no . . ."

She laughed and started the biscuits around. "That's all right, son, I'm a pretty old woman. Not that I still ain't got an eye for a well-set-up young feller," she added, squinting at me out the corners of her eyes.

"Eh . . . yeah . . . yessum."

She looked at me in approval.

"By God, Step, I like your buddy. You boys have had sense enough to stay just boys."

"Aw, nuts," said Step. "We can hold our own

with any man. Don't care if it's liquor or women."

"I ain't saying you ain't a man," corrected Mag. "And I ain't forgetting you done a man's job for me once."

"Nuts," grunted Step.

"Yessir," she said to me. "He sure stood up for me once. You lucky to have a buddy like him."

"Where's all your guns?" asked Step quickly. "Still hunt like you used to?"

"Sure, only it ain't open season on nothing but rabbits and ground hogs now. But speaking of guns, boy, wait till you see the new contraption I got. Had it made special, a four-barrel shotgun. It sure is a honey."

"Hope you can hit a barn door with it," said Step. "For somebody that likes to hunt, you get less than anybody I ever saw."

"That's right," she said reflectively. "I sure can't hit nothing. But how I loves to hear them go off."

The kid had just about stuffed himself by this

66

time. He paused with his cheeks full of biscuit and raised his fingers like they were pistols.

"Bam . . . bam . . . bam . . ." He brought down an imaginary flock of something or other.

Mag laughed loudly and the kid looked pleased with himself.

"He sure is a funny kid," she said. "Where 'd you find him?"

"He ain't funny," said Step, "he's yellow. Can't stand boo."

The kid looked hurt clear through, like Step's attitude was killing him. Anybody could see that he liked Step even more than he did me. Tears gathered in his eyes.

"I not scared."

"Naw, you ain't scared," mocked Step. "Look at you, getting set to bawl now."

Mag and me tried to comfort the kid with soft looks, but Step was scornful of our attempts. He did not let up a bit.

"Aw, let him be," he growled, and suddenly he poked with his fork at the kid's hand. The boy jumped, red muddying the khaki of his face.

"That proves it," cried Step. "Scared to death I was gonna hurt him. He's just yellow."

"That don't prove nothing. Nobody wants to get punched in the hand," said Mag.

"That shows he's scared of everything."

There was a series of sharp cracks from somewhere back of the house. Except Mag, we all started. She grinned.

"Take it easy, boys. It's only Cooper out in the back yard. He likes to pop off with a twenty-two at tin cans."

Step tried to save face: "Let's go out there—that's fun."

"Naw, wait a minute. You got to see my new contraption first." She left the table muttering: "Damn twenty-twos . . . give me something that makes some noise."

68

No sooner had she left the table than I whirled
on Step to ask the question that had been eating
me up:

"What'd she mean, you stood up for her once?"

"Save it . . . Save it . . . Tell you later," he
growled.

"Aw, c'mon, give."

"I said save it."

"Oh, all right." There was no use in pressing him.
"Who's this guy Cooper?"

"Her man."

"Her what?"

"Her man . . . man, stupid."

"But I thought you said she was fifty-three years
old," I gasped.

"Yeah, and you better hope you're good as she is
when you get that old."

"Is he her pimp?"

"Used to be, but now, of course, Mag don't turn
no more tricks. She don't have to. So he just manages
business things for her."

"She sure is a lot of woman. Imagine keeping a man around to sleep with at fifty-three."

"It ain't just that," said Step. "Why, they like each other better than most married folks, I betcha."

Mag came in carrying the gun. It was a beautiful job—silver hammered into the stock and everything. She handed it to Step.

"What you think of that little piece of business?"

"Jeez, you could knock over a whole flock of ducks with this," he exclaimed. "It's heavy as lead."

"Can't let go with but two barrels at a time," explained Mag. "It'd knock you silly."

Step handed the gun across Hi Boy to me. The kid started to reach up and touch it.

"Hands off," said Step. "You might stick your hand on the trigger guard or something and start bawling."

I took the gun and tried to sight down it. Gee, but it was heavy. Took all my strength to hold it level.

70

Nobody had been watching the kid; we were too interested in the gun. Out of the corners of my eyes I might have seen him pick up the fork and thought nothing about it. Hell, we were at a table where there was food—how was I to know he wasn't going to use it to eat with. But there was the fork standing straight up in his hand and the blood oozing up around the prongs that were imbedded in the flesh.

It hadn't been an accident.

He held the hand out to Step. "I not scared."

For a moment we just sat there watching the blood stain the checkered tablecloth a deeper red. The kid's mouth quivered, but he said calmly:

"I not scared of stick hand."

Mag snapped out of it. "What the hell?"

She pulled out the fork. The kid drew in his breath but did not flinch. Ugly little puckery mouths reached for the retreating tines, then the blood began to really flow. Step and me were still just looking.

71

"Well, get the lead out of your feet, one of you guys," cried Mag. "Get the dishpan, some warm water, a towel . . . In there, in the kitchen."

The kid's hand was filthy, so hurt or no hurt Mag washed it with laundry soap. The water in the dishpan was now oxblood. Step and me were scared to death, but Mag didn't pay us any attention.

"Hell, it don't hurt kids to bleed some. 'Sides, can't wrap up all that dirt along with the bandage."

Step held the kid's hand when she put the iodine in the holes. It must have burned something terrible, but the kid didn't cry once.

"Not scared . . . not scared," he said once or twice, when the pain seemed about to get the best of him.

"I'll tell the world you're not," cried Step, after the hand was all tied up.

Step was pitiable in his attempts to put everything right again. He didn't know just what to say, so

72

he and the kid just walked arm in arm through the house. I wouldn't talk to him, but the kid took everything at its face value. He was tops again with Step and that was enough for him. To ease the tension Mag played some old recordings of "The Two Black Crows."

The records were funny but I would not let myself laugh. Step kept looking over at me, as much as to say: "Jesus, you can see I'm sorry as hell." Still, I didn't break down until Mag played a recording of "My Shawl." That was music. The kind that is played in brothels all over the world. The Cuban swing caught us all, and in a moment Step had the kid around the waist and was off on what looked like a tango.

Mag and me howled.

The little feller was just about knocked out on his feet with kindness and attention. He couldn't sit down a second before Step would have thought up some new stunt to do. Finally, as a last gesture,

73

Step decided that he would teach the kid how to shoot. Mag was agreeable but thought it best to use one of Cooper's twenty-twos . . . the shotguns were so heavy.

Cooper was still in the back yard popping away at tin cans. He was thin, slick and high yellow, with enough pomade on his hair to fry a steak. The hair must have been dyed because the morning beard on his face was pure white. Altogether, he looked like a man just recovering from a sickness.

Sure, he would be glad for Step to use one of his guns. Nothing was too good for Step. I wondered again what it was that my buddy had done for these folks.

"Now, here, let me show you," said Step to the kid. He put several tin cans and a couple of bottles on the fence. Then, taking a stand about eighty feet away, he lifted the rifle to his shoulder and sighted along the barrel.

Crack . . .

74

The bullet must have ended up in the middle of the next state somewhere; it certainly didn't meet any interference on the way.

"Yaaaaaa . . ." cried Mag, "an' he says I ain't no shot."

Step gave the gun to Hi Boy.

"You get the general idea," he said.

The kid lifted the gun and without seeming to aim it, fired. One of the bottles shattered, throwing slivers against the sun.

"Jeez, what luck," cried Step, but he spoke out of turn.

Crack . . . Crack . . . Crack . . .

The gun went off just as fast as the kid could cock it, and after each shot there was one less tin can on the fence.

"Gawd, where 'd he learn to shoot like that?" asked Cooper.

We couldn't tell him.

"I shoot 'em good?" asked the kid.

"Where'd you learn that?" I asked.

"I shoot good." He answered his own question. And that was all he would say.

He must have used up a couple of boxes of cartridges proving to us that his accuracy was no accident, and still we wanted him to keep on shooting. Finally Mag put a stop to it.

"Let him rest that hand of his awhile," she said.

When we got ready to go that afternoon, Step took Mag to one side and they talked. The upshot of it was that the kid kept the twenty-two. Mag and Cooper wanted to give Step a shotgun too, but he got around taking it.

Hitting the pavement to Sampson's was fun. We walked along, our stomachs full, our minds easy. The kid pointed his gun this way and that, so it was a miracle that we got out of town without getting into trouble. Once on the highway, Step let him load it and he killed a couple of rabbits before we had gone a half mile. That was enough rabbits, so although we hated to do it we had to take the gun away from him.

We were in sight of the place some time after the sun had started downwards. We must have been a funny sight—two bareheaded fellers with a rabbit apiece slung over their shoulders, and a Mexican kid trailing along singing to a shiny gun held out of his reach:

"Hi boy, hi boy, hi boy, hi . . ."

Did you ever hear a lark whistle in the early morning when everything is fresh and cool? The sound comes from somewhere out in the desert. Of course, the desert here is not the sandy waste that you would think of as being a desert. The purple and green of the thistle and sage, the stretches of cactus, mesquite and tumbleweed make it sort of a big back yard of your house. The lark sings from somewhere in this back yard. His whistle is just as long as the chorus to a cowboy song . . . and has more melody in it. That was what woke us up on the morning of the first day at Sampson's. That, and the frying smell of the rabbits that Hi Boy had killed the day before.

The three of us had slept on a little screened-in back porch. There was a bed for Step and me and a cot for the kid. It was better than being in the house for us who were used to sleeping under just any little piece of sky. The only real bedrooms in the one-story frame building were for Sampson and his daughter Anna.

Anna wasn't bad-looking and she wasn't good-looking. I guess she was like any other late teen-age country girl . . . a little plump and a little giggly. Just a towheaded kid, except for her eyes. They were deep with that same quiet saneness that marked Sampson's.

The day we arrived Step had been fresh with Anna. She had been apologizing for the lack of space, saying that the workers who came at apple-picking time usually slept under a tent pitched in the orchard. Step had said that he would not want to crowd Sampson, which was polite enough; but then he asked if she kicked in her sleep. She had already answered in the negative before the meaning of the question dawned on her. Tossing her head, she had flounced off.

I was afraid that she was going to tell her father, but Step had grinned at my fears.

"Don't be a chump. She's been buried out here in the desert just waiting for some guy to come along and get fresh with her."

Maybe he knew what he was talking about. Sampson hadn't given any sign of being sore at us yet.

The slam of a screen door close by was like a pistol shot in the morning air. Then Anna's voice:

"Here, chick . . . chick . . . chick . . ."

The kid got out of bed and went over to the screen. Not having any underwear he had slept in the suit he was born with. I nudged Step. It was a shame to laugh about something like that but we couldn't help it. And it was all right, because the kid didn't know what we were laughing at.

"See . . . see . . . *¡mire, luego!*" called the kid.

We hopped out of the sheets. Maybe the kid could have gotten a laugh at our expense, but he was too excited by what he saw in the yard.

At first we thought he was talking about the mountains; through the clear air they had traveled almost within hock-and-spitting distance. Then Step grabbed me by the arm.

"Jeez, will you look at that guy!" he cried.

It was something to get excited about. The wild pheasants were in the yard feeding with the chickens. Step was pointing at the big cock in the bunch. Fully as big as any rooster, his tail and brilliant wings chocked with color and vitality, he lorded it over all the flock.

"Boy, what I wouldn't give for a shot at him."

No sooner had Step spoken than the kid grabbed

up the rifle and cocked it. He was going to shoot through the screen. Step knocked up the barrel.

"You want to get us locked up? Can't shoot 'em out of season."

"Yeah, we're just crazy about holes in the screen too," I remarked.

While we were talking to him I noticed Anna at the foot of the backdoor stoop.

"Duck, quick," I warned.

She had on a bonnet that covered her face, but I was deathly afraid that at any minute she might turn and see us. That, together with Step's freshness the day before, would just about finish our stay at Four Mile Farm.

"My, what a nice morning," said Step loudly. He was acting like he didn't know she was there.

"C'mon, Step, please." I pulled at his arm.

"Boy, this air makes a feller feel like breathing," he declared even more loudly, and cupping his hands, he beat on his bare chest.

81

It was awful, expecting her to turn around before I could get him away from the screen. Safely out of sight of the yard, I angrily turned on him:

"Whazza matter? You trying to get us thrown out of here on our ears?"

He regarded me with disgust.

"I see I got to learn you everything just like you was Hi Boy. Just suppose it was you out there by the steps and somebody talked as loud as we were talking. Wouldn't you have turned around to see what it was all about . . . or to say good morning?"

"Maybe she didn't hear us."

"The hell you say she didn't," he cried. "She had been peeking and knew we were raw. That's why she played mum."

"Aw, you're always thinking dirty."

He looked at me pityingly. "Jeez, how can you be so simple and live?" That was his final comment.

Breakfast was a quick affair, all of us eating at a big table in the kitchen. There was a grizzled old hired hand there too. His home was in the tool shed. Anna brought on the rabbits. They were cooked crisp and ate like chicken, only not as tender. Both Step and me praised the cooking, but not once would Anna look at us. That was strange.

At the sheep pen the hired man, Orlando was his name, gave us both a big plug of tobacco. I didn't know what the tobacco was for but I took it and bit off a hunk. The kid sat on the fence watching us chew. His hand was still sore, so for the first two or three days it was arranged for him to keep the house supplied with rabbits and watch for a hawk that had been carrying away the chickens.

I soon found out what the tobacco was for. All the lambs in the pen were to be castrated. This was done with a knife, but the final operation was made with the teeth. That was so the wound would heal clean, according to Orlando. And somewhere I remembered hearing that tobacco was a good antiseptic.

We alternated on the biting, the other two holding. Even so, by noontime I was sick as hell. Partly
from the lambs squirting in my face and the blood
taste, but mostly from the strong cut-plug tobacco.
I was glad to wash up and get ready for lunch, even
though I knew I wasn't going to be able to eat any.

The work had not bothered Step. He had done
that kind of labor before. As we doused ourselves
in cold hard water the kid kept worrying him for a
chew of the tobacco. He told the kid to go away
and forget it but the advice was disregarded. So he
gave him a piece of the plug. That left two of us
sitting in the shade behind the tool house while the
others were eating lunch.

Sampson came out and talked to us after a bit.
He raised three types of Delicious apples, he explained; and the trees that bore each type had to be
pruned differently. He had spent the morning in
the orchards. He loved apple-growing, but the fruit
market was so unsteady that he had decided to try

sheep on the side. Especially since the government alloted free grazing land.

"Wish apples were as stable as mutton," he said. "Why, back just a few years ago we let the fruit fall to the ground and rot. Cost more to pick, crate and ship than it brought on the market."

"That was a shame," I said. "There ain't never enough apples for the poor kids who ain't got the price of one."

"Lot of farmers around here chopped out their orchards on account of that . . . but I couldn't have done it. Why, I love my orchards like another man loves a woman. You don't quit a woman because she don't come up to the mark two or three seasons. And besides, I was four years in college and the better part of my life learning how to raise the best Delicious apples in this here valley."

"Everybody likes apples. It's a funny thing when a man can't make money when he's got something that everybody likes."

"Well, that's the way it is with apples, son. When you got them the price is down. When you haven't got them the price is up. You don't make anything to speak of, either way."

"Don't guess I'd ever make a farmer," I said. "I'd sell the land and get a job in the city."

"Oh, I don't think you would. Not if you owned a little piece of land."

"Fellers that own a little piece of land don't ever get rich," I told him. "Leastways, I never heard of any."

"Reckon that's right," he said, "but there's something about growing things that gets you."

"Guess you'd sooner grow apples than be president," I said.

"Don't know about that. Can't say how it feels to be president, but an apple sure is a beautiful thing. Makes a man think about guns and revolutions when he sees them rotting on the ground."

"Guess so. Ain't the government doing nothing about that?"

"All they can, I guess. But sometimes I think we'd be better off if they took a rest and let God run the world a little."

"I sure hope we'll be able to help you out some," I said.

"You know, I didn't really think you boys was going to follow me on here," he smiled, "but I'm right glad you came. Sorta took a fancy to you fellers. 'Specially Hi Boy, here." He knuckled the kid's head.

The kid did not look up. He took it as a natural thing that he should be liked.

"I been in this part of the country lots of times, following the big fifty-mule combines through the wheat fields," I said. "Reckon I'm sorry I never run across Four Mile Farm before this."

"Like old times to have some boys around the place," he said, and looked far away at a big mountain that seemed to loom just behind the farthest orchard. "Used to sit around here many an evening

87

with Mary. . . . We'd look at that mountain. The boys would be off somewhere, but you could hear them shouting and kidding one another."

I didn't say anything. I could see that he was living over again something that must have meant a lot to him. The mood was broken by the kid throwing and shouting at a chicken that had strayed behind the shed. Sampson got up quickly.

"Reckon I'd better finish that south orchard while there's sun," he said gruffly.

Later on, when we were in the sheep pen once more, I asked Orlando about Sampson.

"Shore, he had some boys," said Orlando. "Four of the finest lads ever growed in this here valley. They was the first in these parts to volunteer when Uncle Sam jined in the scrap overseas. Funny thing about it was that none of 'em was killed by gunfire. They all died o' some kinda sickness while they was in a training camp."

"Mary was his wife, huh?" I prompted.

88

"Shore was . . . Broke her all to pieces when those boys blew in their chips. Didn't last more 'n five year after'ards. I reckon Sampson might 've followed her if it hadn't been for the little gal Anna. She weren't no more 'n born at the time. That gal and apples is all that keeps him on this here earth."

Late that night Step and me rolled cigarettes and talked. Everyone else about the place was in bed, but the night was pleasantly cool and we were seated on the top step out of reach of the rattlesnakes that lived underneath the back porch, so we just naturally had to discuss things.

"How long you figger we're going to stay here, Step?"

"Got itchy foot already?" he laughed. "I told you sheep wasn't no picnic."

"Naw, it ain't that. I just want to know."

"Well, I'd say 'bout a month at the most, I guess."

"He's a pretty swell feller," I remarked.

"Sampson?"

"Yeah."

"Guess he is, at that."

"Bet you didn't know that he used to have four boys just about as old as us when they died," I said.

"That's tough."

"He says that it's like old times to have us around the place."

"Guess so."

"We'll be gone in 'bout a month, you say?"

"Yeah, how come you to ask that again?"

"Oh, I don't know. . . . He'll be sorry to see us go, I betcha."

"Say, you ain't getting soft, are you?" he inquired. "You ain't hinting that we ought to stay here?"

"Naw . . . Naw, nothing like that," I assured him.

"That's all right, then. You had me guessing for a minute."

90

"Boy, you sure can get me wrong," I told him.

"Why, we ain't seen half the world yet," he said. "We ain't never had one of them island women, either."

"You mean the kind that wear the grass and wiggles their stomachs?"

"Yeah, like at carnivals," he said. Then: "Where do they hang out, anyway?"

"Oh, I don't know," I said vaguely.

"It don't matter; if we keep on traveling we're bound to run across them. Why, when it comes to going to bed, I bet they'd make a gal like Anna look sick."

Everything in me held motionless for a second. Step must have sensed that something was wrong.

"What's eating you?"

"About Anna," I said. "She's only a kid."

"So what? She's old enough to play around like she knows what it's all about."

"She ain't old enough, Step. You got to leave her alone."

"What you mean I got to leave her alone?" he asked harshly.

For once I did not give in to him. I knew what I meant and was ready to back it up. Our faces were not six inches apart. I would not be stared down.

"This is the time we either got to agree or part company," I told him.

Suddenly he laughed. "Aw, who ever said I was going to bother her, softie?" And he slapped me on the shoulder.

"All right, I'm soft, but I want you to promise."

"Aw, forget it."

"You got to promise."

"Hell, I promise." He got to his feet. "Hope that makes you feel better, mama."

Long after he had gone to bed I sat there looking in the direction of the farthest orchard to where the big mountain would be if the air was clear tomorrow. I could almost hear the old hired hand say: "That gal and apples is all that keeps him on this here earth."

We were a full week with the sheep—getting another batch ready for shipment, staking out the ewes at feeding time so that the lambs could find their real mamas, helping Orlando get the main flock ready to travel to the government pasture land. . . . Step and me gave a hearty cheer when the old hired hand and his woolly pets herded by a sheep dog were gone.

Step was keeping his promise, too, although the strain was telling on him. I helped him by calling him away whenever Anna came around. She seemed to sense his resolution and resent it, and whenever she wasn't deep in some love-story magazine she was switching around in front of him. One day in the orchards he almost forgot himself for a minute when she kissed him, he told me, but by concentrating on everything unpleasant that had ever happened to him he got mad enough to break away. I hadn't counted on that much will power in Step.

Sampson and the kid were buddies almost at first sight. Now they were together all the time. Before sunup they would be out hunting rabbits; in the evenings they jabbered in Spanish as they walked in the orchards; and at night Sampson would sit with him on the porch and try to enlarge his knowledge of English. Most of these English lessons would end with the teacher and the pupil spouting such fluent Spanish that my ear could not distinguish one word from another.

Step and me were pretty busy in the truck garden while waiting for a small gang plow to be used to break the ground in the new orchard for the planting of subsidiary crops. Sometimes we found time to go out with Sampson and the kid, and on week ends we would ride the truck into town and raise

94

hell. Still, I could see that the place was beginning to get on Step's nerves. He always grouched a lot when the urge to move on was about to hit him. Just any day I expected to have him suddenly say: "Get on your coat, we got to get going." That's the way he always left a place—in a hurry. We might have collected our pay and left without anything at all happening if the kid hadn't been troubled with his hand.

The holes left by the tines of the fork had healed over all right, but there must have been some infection on the inside, because one morning the whole hand was red and swollen.

Sampson bathed the hand in hot water but that didn't do any good; so on the third morning when the hand had not gone down, he told us to take the truck and go into town with the kid. The doctor there took care of all his people and got paid by the year.

The kid hadn't been far from the place since we

got there, so when he heard that he was going to town in the truck he sang like one of those larks. The only thing that soured the trip for me was Anna being along, but she could handle the truck better than anybody else so there was nothing I could say.

We were pretty gay all the way in, singing Western ballads and laughing at any and everything. The kid's "Hi boy" rang almost continuously from the time we left the farm to the moment we pulled up in front of the doc's office. About five minutes of waiting in the outer office sobered us all up, however. The place smelled of ether and operations. I was glad that it wasn't me who had to face the doc.

"This isn't so good," said the doc as he peered over his gold-rimmed specs at the hand.

"What you think, Doc?" asked Step.

"Ummmmmm . . ." He pressed the hand here and there in a way to make the kid wince.

"How bad is it?" I asked.

"Yeah, what you think, Doc?"

96

"Should have brought him in before this," snapped the doc. "Whose kid is he?"

He had asked Anna, but she didn't know how to answer.

"He kind of belongs to us," said Step.

"We sorta adopted him," I explained.

"Well, coming from Sampson is good enough for me. I'll have to lance this, of course." He dropped a thin knife into a steaming pan.

"You ain't going to cut nothing off, are you, Doc?" cried Step.

The kid whimpered.

"No, no, son. It's not that serious. I just mean to open it up and get some of that pus out."

"Sure . . . sure, that's what I thought . . ." faltered Step.

"No need at all of you staying here," said the doctor. "Why not just leave the boy and come back in an hour or so?"

The kid looked around as if he had been condemned. You could see that if he hadn't been afraid of Step's displeasure he would have cried.

"I'll stay here," declared Step. "You and Anna can take a walk or something."

We left them there holding hands while the doctor washed up. Anna did not want to stand in front of shop windows, so we wandered down to the railroad station. All the time we were walking I felt that she had something to say to me . . . and we hadn't been at the station more than half an hour before she started in.

"You and him been traveling together a long time?" she asked, seating herself on the railing of the station yard.

"Few years, I guess."

"Oh, I thought maybe you knew something about where he came from and all."

"Maybe I do." I really didn't know anything much but I wasn't telling her that.

"Ain't a secret, is it?"

"Don't know. Maybe he wouldn't like me to talk about him to girls he only just met."

She settled back on the railing and smiled, her eyes that sane way that made you forget she was just a giggly girl.

"You're against my liking him," she stated.

"It ain't that."

"What is it, then? Ever since you fellers came to Pop's farm you been steering him away from me."

It was embarrassing to have a girl talk that frankly, even though I admired her for it. I couldn't tell her the truth outright, either—that to Step, having a woman was just about as sacred a thing as washing his hands.

"You must have some reason," she insisted.

"I guess maybe you're beginning to fall for him," I evaded, desperately twisting at a turf of grass between my feet.

"Would there be anything wrong about that?"

"Most of them do," I said, "and then we usually move along somewheres."

She laughed.

"Well, maybe it's 'cause I'm kinda soft for your old man," I said, now in a stew of embarrassment. She surprised me by patting my hand.

"You're a hell of a good pal, Ed." It didn't sound funny to hear her swear. "But you wouldn't know what it means to be a girl and not be able to bum around the country or do anything exciting or romantic. Maybe you don't know what it is to have a father who thinks about you like—like one of his apples."

"How's that?"

"Well, he can't stand to see any of his apples fall on the ground . . . and he won't let his 'little girl' mix with any of the pickers or the young people around town who get high at dances."

"You don't have any friends?"

"Yeah, the thirteen-year-old kids of a few hand-picked farmers."

"Maybe he knows more about it than you do," I told her.

"But he don't know how it is to have a feller like Step come along—who looks at you like the fellers on the covers of the love-story magazines." She glanced at me to see how I was taking it. "Don't know why I'm telling you all this. I guess folks just start talking and before they know it they've said more than they were going to say."

"Guess I know how you feel," I said.

"Maybe you don't," she cried. "It ain't that I want to do anything bad. It's just that I'm tired of being an apple when I'm a woman."

Poor little kid, I thought. She don't want to do anything bad. Maybe she thinks that Step will just kiss her hand and neck her in some garden like they do in the magazines. Why, she'd be all done for before she knew what was happening.

A passenger train blew by just then, one of the new streamliners—all metal and shine, blinding in the sunlight. Anna looked after the train and sighed.

"Wish I was on that train. When I was a little bit

of a thing we used to holler when we saw a train; that made it yours, if you hollered first."

"Oh, it ain't so much fun on the cushions," I told her.

We sat there chewing grass blades. Both of us were at ease because we felt like we'd confessed something. There was no longer any need to strain at the main thread of our conversation . . . we had time to think up little unconnected side issues.

"You like honey?" she asked.

"I like it on flapjacks."

"So do I. I wish I was on that train eating honey and flapjacks."

"Probably charge you ten bucks," I said. "I've been in those diners."

"You have?"

"Sure . . . Oh, sure, lots of times," I lied.

"Did you have flapjacks?"

"Naw, what 'd be the use? They wouldn't know how to make 'em—that is, with sour milk."

"I think he likes Hi Boy better than anybody else," she said smoothly, as if she was still talking about trains.

"Who?"

"I mean Step."

"I guess so. He don't care nothing about girls. That is, one's as good as another to him."

She looked sharply at me. "It's funny that you're his buddy and talk about him like that."

"That ain't nothing to say; it's true."

"I don't believe it," she declared. "And what's more, I think I'll show you where you're wrong."

"Naw, don't do anything like that," I said.

"He says a lot of nice things. I don't think he'd go out of his way to say them if he didn't mean it."

"That's just a line. You wouldn't take your hand and stir up that nest of rattlesnakes under your back doorstep, would you?"

"Why, no. Anyway, snakes underneath the porch are good luck."

"Well, don't go stirring up a man, 'cause you're only a kid and you're liable to get bit."

She laughed at me again.

Hi Boy's hand was all bandaged when Anna and me got back to the doctor's. As soon as we walked in Step started running off at the mouth:

"Jeez, you should 've seen it. Why, when the doc opened that hand and squeezed, the juice must have spouted that high." He held his hand up about seven feet. "Jeez, it was just like one of those cobbler pies on the inside."

"All fix now," said the kid, showing the hand.

"You lose that bandage and get any dirt in that wound, and you won't have any more hand," the doc told him.

"Sure, sure. I'll watch him, Doc," promised Step.

"Sure . . . he watch," said the kid.

"Tell Sampson to send him back here in a week

or so," said the doc to Anna. "And by the way, how is the old sheep nurse making out?"

"He's doing all right," she said. "Apples look like they're going to be good this year, and he just shipped out a couple of carloads of mutton on the hoof."

"Have to up the ante on him then," laughed the doc.

We would not have thought of going to a movie if some friends of Sampson's hadn't been getting into a parked car just outside the doc's office. Anna got the idea to have these friends drop Hi Boy by the farm and tell Sampson where we were going.

The friends were willing—they were passing right by Four Mile. It was the kid who did not like the plan. I couldn't blame him for not wanting to miss the picture, but because of his hand we thought it best for him to be at the farm. We finally had to tell him that kids weren't allowed in picture shows on Saturday.

The movie was one of those good old westerns, the kind that you sit through twice. Throughout the whole four hours we whooped and hollered. When the bad guys had the smiling young feller tied up, woolly pants and all, we booed and hooted; and when the hero saved the girl from a herd of stampeding cows and captured the bad guys, we cheered.

It was evening when we came out into the fresh air again.

"Let's drive down by the tracks and wait for the early moon," suggested Anna. "It's too nice an evening to go home right away."

We were willing.

Step and me knew a few girls in town. We had met them on our first Saturday night in Yakima. It was only natural for me to pick up one of them to help with the waiting. I picked the nicest one I could think of, which wasn't saying much, because I didn't want Anna to be out with just any little biddy.

The four of us were pretty noisy for awhile, but after the moon came out the talk and laughter died. The girl I had picked up, Belle was her name, dragged me around to the back of the truck. I didn't notice what Step was doing. I was too excited by the feel of Belle's warm breasts. After a long time I did remember to look towards the front seat. Step was kissing Anna; but I drowned my qualms by thinking that, after all, a little petting wouldn't do the girl any hurt, and I would see that it didn't go any farther than that. I attended to my own woman.

"What say we get a bottle of Chinese saki and make a real party out of it?" called Step after about an hour of petting.

That would be fine, thought Belle.

"No, we better not," I said.

"Aw, please, Ed," said Anna. "You remember, I've never been on a party."

"Well, okay," I agreed. It would be better, any-how, for us to be doing something. This petting was

107

getting out of control. Maybe after Step had had a little of the rice wine he would take Anna home and come back to get him a good-time girl like Belle.

I didn't want to go by Mag's, because if Sampson ever found out he'd kill us; but we didn't have any money and Mag was the only person who would give us credit.

"Besides, we won't have to go in," argued Step. "She can just bring it out to the truck."

We drove around the long way and approached the back of Mag's house through the alleyways. Step got out and walked up to the screen door. Mag must have been in the kitchen for she rushed out before he had a chance to knock. I could tell that she was insisting that we come inside. I was all set to refuse as she and Step approached the truck.

"Whyn't you children come on in for a few minutes?" she hollered. "Why, nobody'll know you there."

"Aw, we got to hurry back to the farm," I said.

"Just for a minute. I'd sorta be pleased to take a drink with you."

Anna whispered to me: "Let's go in—it'd be fun."

"Sure, let's go in," said Belle.

I hesitated.

"Maybe you ashamed to bring your ladyfolks in my house," said Mag.

Step put his hand on Mag's arm.

"It ain't nothing like that," he said. "Ed's just worried about getting back to the place." He looked meaningfully at me. "Don't be a heel, c'mon."

A couple of minutes later we were all sitting around the kitchen table. Cooper took several milk bottles full of saki out of a closet and filled up enough water glasses to go around.

"Ought to be some kind of toast said before we take the spider off this wine," he said.

Step began: "To anything on wheels that can take a man where he ain't been before . . ." We started to raise our glasses, but Mag stopped us with a gesture. Her dirty toasts were famous among the guys that hung around the poolrooms. Maybe we were going to hear a new one, I thought.

"I'm right proud to have you children in my house," she began, "and sooner or later, I'm going to drink to each one of you. But first I want to drink to this young feller here, Step. If it wasn't for him old Mag wouldn't be sitting here now."

We emptied the glasses. Rice wine is like that— you can drink it like water.

"Aw, stuff," grumbled Step.

"What did he do?" I asked. "He wouldn't tell me."

"Sure, let us in on it," said Belle.

"We got a right to know what we're drinking to," I said.

"Guess that's right," said Mag.

Step jumped up and took one of the bottles from the table.

"Hell, I ain't going to sit here and be made no hero." He pulled Anna to her feet. "C'mon, sugar, le's go up front and play some records."

Mag poured another round of drinks and went over to sit in Cooper's lap. We could hear Step's laughter mingled with the trumpet runs of "My Shawl." It sounded like they were dancing in the parlor. Maybe I was crazy to think that Anna and Step couldn't have a little fun together without getting into trouble. I found myself feeling glad because Step was a good dancer and could show her a good time. I was just as pleased as if it was me who guided her in the Cuban rhythm. Feeling like that about a girl was disturbing.

"Hope Cooper don't mind my telling this," said Mag. "Anyway, it was long time ago . . . bygones is bygones. He didn't have no reason to get worked up over this Hunky, but everybody here at the place was drunk and maybe it seemed to him like I was making a play for the guy."

"You mean he was jealous of some other feller?" asked Belle.

"Seems funny to you, don't it, that folks like us can get the wind up over each other? That's because you don't understand. Business is business, and that's all right; but to make a play for somebody just for what he's got in his pants, that's a horse of another color. I reckon Cooper felt like any other man'd feel if he thought his woman was hot for another guy."

"And I ain't sure yet you wasn't," growled Cooper.

Mag looked at him fondly. "Jeez, but you beat the hell out of me. I couldn't move around good for a week." She paused to light his cigar. "But to get on with the story, in the ruckus that followed this guy was stabbed a couple of times. Ain't nobody could say it was Cooper did it. He didn't have no knife on him when the sheriff come. They didn't have no evidence to take him to the lockup, but they did."

"Had to put me back on the street, though," said Cooper. "Even the Hunky that got cut couldn't say for sure it was me."

"That's getting ahead of the story," said Mag. "It was while he was in jail that the real trouble started. That's where Step comes in. He had been here in the house that night, but of course everybody cleared out after the cutting. And out of all the guys I've given free drinks to, he was the only one who was man enough to save me from being rid out of town on a rail . . . or worse."

As Mag stopped to take a drink Belle came over and plopped down on my knees. I had just finished my fourth straight glass of wine. The stuff tasted like nothing, but like a bolt of lightning it had knocked the starch out of me all at once. It was all I could do to hold up under Belle's weight.

Thin and distant now, Mag's voice started up again: "Step heard the bastards in some joint plotting to get me. Would have, too, if he hadn't gone to get the sheriff. The mob was bashing in the front and back doors when he brings the law on the scene. Course I had my old shotgun aimed straight down the hall. Almost let the law have it when he pushed open the busted door. Funny too, 'cause I never thought I'd be glad to see a sheriff."

Cooper shoved Mag out of his lap and stood up. "That wasn't the first time the folks around here has tried to run us out of town. Ever so often they get a spell of cleaning up. Funny thing about it is that the very bastards who start trouble are the ones who are sneaking down here every chance they get."

"I don't hold nothing against them," said Mag. "It ain't like the South where I come from. Didn't make no difference that it was a white man got cut up. They always just as ready to run white out of town as well as black, once they get riled."

"I ain't been closer south than Walla Walla," said Belle, wiggling around on my knees.

"It don't make no difference where you go," said

114

Cooper, "they always hating somebody somewhere. All along from Texas through New Mexico they hate Mexes worse 'n a snake; down in lower California they get like mad dogs if you mention Japs; I ain't never been far east, but they say that out there everybody hates everybody else."

"What you reckon makes people like that?" puzzled Mag.

Nobody could answer that one.

My attention was distracted by Belle who just couldn't sit still on my knees. I wanted to push her off to the floor.

"Sit still, will you?" I whispered.

Making as if to whisper back she leaned over and bit my ear. Then with her head on my shoulder she slid astraddle one of my legs. Her thin summer dress was pushed up around her hips.

Cooper looked at us with a grin.

"Looks like you got something on your hands."

"Yeah."

"Some legs."

High as I was, I could see that he was not interested in Belle's legs; but it seemed as though he
wanted Mag to think he was. While seeming to gaze
at us, he was really watching Mag out of the corners
of his eyes.

The night was warm, and the weight on my knee
was just so much hot flesh. One of my legs had gone
to sleep, and little pinprickles were beginning to
run up and down my side. The breath in my face
was heavy with wine scent. I was in misery.

"Been a long time since we had one of these drinking and talking sessions," said Cooper, still seeming
to be intent on Belle's legs.

Mag got up and pulled him away from the table.

"Reckon we talked enough for one night. Let's go
in the front and listen to the vic."

He wanted to stay, but Mag insisted. He gave me
a wink as he left. Mag leaned toward us.

"You kids want a room for the night?"

Belle poked at my ear again with her wet tongue.

"We got to be getting on . . . must be late." My own voice sounded so far away that it startled me.

Belle pouted: "Betcha Step don't want to go."

"He probably found him a room already," said Mag.

The wine ran away from my head in a flood.

"Where's Step?" I yelled.

"Where you think he'd be?" said Mag.

"Where's Step?" I asked again.

"You must be high," said Mag. "Thought I just told you."

I listened for the victrola. I could hear "My Shawl," but it seemed to be inside my own head. On deadened legs I jerked myself erect, spilling Belle underneath the table.

"Watch what you're doing," she cried.

"Got to find Step."

Pushing past Mag I ran into the parlor.

"Now what the hell's eating him?" I heard Mag say.

There was nobody but Cooper in the dark parlor. Stretched out on the davenport, a cigarette illuminated his yellowish lips.

"Most likely upstairs," he said before I could speak. He must have heard us talking in the kitchen.

I made a lot of noise stumbling up the stairs. At the top landing, bewildered by the dark, I halted.

"Step, Step," I said uncertainly.

A door halfway down the hall opened and a dim light showed up his face . . . terrified. I ran to him. "Anna?"

He could not answer. His features seemed to be scrambled up. I knew that look. Once a stevedore working shoulder to shoulder with me had gotten his leg caught between the pier and a rolling freighter. There was that same look on his face as his leg was pulped.

Shot through with a fear that left me calm and icy, I followed Step into the room. Over his shoulder I could see the head of a bed and Anna's face pale

against a white pillow. Her moans made little clicking noises as they were forced up through her
spittle. The sheet tucked underneath her chin was
wet with spittle.

"What's wrong with her?"

I shook him.

"What'd you do to her?"

As I forced myself to lean over and shake her, I
could see the water from her eyes running across
both cheekbones into her massed hair. The wet face
flopped from side to side. Clumsily I gathered up a
corner of the sheet and tried to dry her eyes. It was
no use.

"What're we going to do?"

"To do . . . to do . . ." Step echoed.

"Call somebody, quick," I cried.

"Wait," he said. "A doctor. That's it . . . we got
to get a doctor."

The words seemed to penetrate to the girl. She
raised her head and in her eyes there was a fear
more powerful than pain.

"No . . . no . . . don't . . . please . . ."

"The doc's got to be a good feller; he's got to keep his mouth shut," said Step. "We can't just let her lie here."

"Maybe Mag . . . ?" I suggested.

"Yeah, the way she fixed the kid's hand. Hell, no."

"We'll both get shot up." I grabbed his arm.

"No . . . no," Anna was sobbing.

I relaxed my grip.

"Go ahead; what the hell's the difference?"

Mag strode into the room as Step started to rush out. Holding Step by the slack of his shirt she glanced at the bed, then closed the door behind her. I was surprised at her strength.

"Where you running to?" she asked softly.

"Turn me loose," cried Step, struggling.

"Take it easy now," she said.

"He's got to get a doctor," I cried.

She cowed us with a great contempt.

"So you going to get me in bad just because a

damn little virgin got treated too rough. Don't lose your heads. She ain't going to die. Ain't nothing wrong with her that I ain't fixed up before."

Step started to stammer out something, but Mag stopped him with a snort: "Huh, don't be no fool. I been taking care of women all of my life. Got two houses full right here in town. This is something I know all about."

While we stood undecided, Mag pushed us out into the hall and closed the door in our faces.

"Send Belle up here. Tell her to bring some ice out of the box," she called through the closed door.

We went downstairs.

Belle took the news calmly.

"Aw, quit worrying; it probably ain't much. I seen the same thing happen before when a dumb guy tries to mix drinks and virgins."

Puffing feverishly on our cigarettes, Step and me sat in the dark parlor. Through the smoke I caught a whiff of the dog's tail. I wished that I had something to finger while waiting. Cooper started to whistle in a low monotone and I had to think hard about something or go crazy. From the kitchen was reflected just enough light for me to make out my buddy's harsh profile. The beak nose and the unruly hair shooting up from his forehead made of his profile a strange desperate bird in flight. I had an impulse to laugh. Suppose his head were to fly away. The desire to laugh almost burst my throat, but I held myself. Somehow, he sensed that I was watching him.

"I know what you're thinking . . . but don't say it."

"I wasn't thinking nothing."

"You're a liar, but keep your trap shut."

I hadn't actually been thinking about what he had done, but deep inside me there was a feeling so intense that I couldn't distinguish it from the kind of thrill you get riding the roller coasters at a fair. Instead of being mad, I wanted to beg his pardon. I just couldn't understand myself.

"Step."

"Yeah."

"I ain't holding no hard feelings about you not keeping your promise."

"So you ain't holding no grudge. All is forgiven. Well, rah-rah-rah for you."

"Aw, I didn't mean it like that."

"Shut up."

"You think she's going to be all right?"

"How should I know?"

"Maybe we'll have to get out of town."

"Shut up, I told you. Keep your trap shut."

The couch squeaked under Cooper as he gave a chuckle.

"Ain't no use in you guys getting all brittle. You ain't in no real trouble yet."

"What you mean?"

"Well, Mag can fix the girl up so she'll be better 'n new . . . but the thing is, will the girl keep her mouth shut?"

"She don't want her paw to know about this any more than we do," I told him.

"I wasn't meaning that. I was thinking about the law."

"The cops?"

"Yeah, they can put you under the jailhouse for rape."

"What do you mean, rape?" snapped Step.

"She's under age, ain't she? Well, that's rape on the books. And if she talks, we'll all go to the hoosegow."

"She won't say nothing," said Step.

"Maybe not, but all the same, we'd better leave this town quick," I said.

Step was quiet for a long time before he spoke.

"We ain't running out on her before she gets home. And we ain't running out on Hi Boy neither."

Anna looked all right when we came to take her out to the truck. They had washed her face and combed her hair, and if it hadn't been for the puffy eyes and the old housecoat wrapped around her, you never could have guessed what she had been through.

"Hello, Anna."

"How you feeling?"

It was an awkward moment, and we had felt like we should say something. I don't know what there was in what we said that should have made her cry.

Mag put her hands on her hips and gave us merry hell.

"Well, you two stupid lugs. What're you trying to do? Trying to make her feel bad? Don't you guys have sense enough to know when to keep your mouths shut? Don't stand there, pick her up. It might start again if she trys to walk right away."

Between us, on crossed hands, we carried Anna out to the truck. Step supported her in the back, and with no thought of Belle I hopped into the driver's seat. Mag thrust a package onto the seat beside me.

"It's her clothes. Drop them out somewhere."

"Okay." I was in a rush to get away.

"Whatever story you're going to tell, get it straight before you get there," screamed Mag as we started up.

The open road was so dark that it seemed like we were roaring along and getting no place. Ordinarily, Step and me would have had hundreds of ideas in fifteen minutes, but with only about a quarter mile to go, the best story we could work out was the old stalled-car gag. Step was trying to coach Anna.

"It'll be dark, and maybe he won't notice your clothes. And if he asks anything, just say the car broke down. Got it? The car broke down."

Within sight of the lighted house I began to get worried. Stopping the car, I threw the package into a ditch and turned to look at Anna. She was stony-faced now . . . straight and staring numbly into the glow of the dashboard light.

"Anna. Anna, do you hear me?" I called.

"Yes."

"What are you going to say when Sampson asks you why we're out so late?"

"Don't know . . ."

"Yes, you do," cried Step. "The car broke down . . . The car broke down."

She didn't answer.

"Look here," I said. "You ain't got no kick coming. So I was trying to steer him away from you . . . So he looks like the fellers on the love-story magazines . . . So you're tired of being an apple . . . All right, you got what you asked for."

She was crying again.

"Lay off," said Step.

"Sure, I'll lay off, but she's got to stick by us. She did what a woman does, now she's got to stay a woman. Can't go running to her old man again, like she was a baby."

"I'll say it," she sobbed. "The car broke down."

"That's right, kid. I didn't mean to be tough, but,

Jeez, all you get out of this is a good licking. Step and me stand to get shot up or sent to prison."

She put her face up against Step's shirt and must have gotten him all wet with her tears. It seemed like she wanted to cling there all night, so I gave Step the sign to break it up.

Just before we got to the house there was a distant roll of thunder. I looked at the sky. No moon, but the stars were all in place. The thunder rolled again . . . peal followed peal. It was eerie as hell to have the thunder bark out of a clear sky. It was like a giant dog away somewhere roaring out his crazy heart.

"You suppose it's gonna rain?" asked Step.

"Ain't a cloud nowheres," I said.

"Never heard thunder without rain or clouds."

"Well," I said, "if it rains out of a clear sky, you can bet your boots somebody up there has gone haywire."

Sampson came to meet us as we rolled into the yard. Hurriedly, I switched off the truck lights.

"Hallo."

"Hallo," called back Step. "Guess you thought we weren't coming back."

"What kept you?"

"Had a little trouble on the road," I said.

He looked through the darkness toward his daughter.

"You all right, Anna?"

The thunder rolled again, and the wire fence took up the vibration and hummed with it.

I heard Anna stumble as she lowered herself from the truck, and I held my breath. Then came a laugh and a voice as free of trouble as an April afternoon:

"No need for you to wait up for me, Paw. The car broke down on the road. Ed fixed it." And as she went through the darkness toward the house: "I'm dead tired. Good night, everybody."

Declining Sampson's invitation to sit out awhile, we took the truck around to the shed. We both had been under a strain for a long time. Now we were ready to drop in our tracks.

"Say, I forgot to ask him if it was going to storm," said Step.

I listened for the thunder.

"Naw, guess it ain't."

The next day was Sunday. Nobody worked on Sunday. When it was hardly light I heard Sampson get up to let the chickens out to scratch, but he went back to his room. Hi Boy, who always beat the sun out of bed, tried to rouse Step and me. His Mexican prattle was mixed up with my dreams.

The heat of the sun finally woke me up. I could see the kid sitting cross-legged on his cot, playing some kind of game with himself. I couldn't understand the words, but it must have been a good game. He would laugh softly every now and then. Refusing to let my mind entirely wake up, I became absorbed in watching him. A beautiful sight there in the sunshine—the light a rich glow on his tawny skin, the heavy black hair over his little jet eyes almost hiding them. In that moment he was a pocket-size edition of a priest laughing over his beads, saying his saints on his fingers. I wanted Step to see him like that.

"Whazza matter? Whazza matter?" grunted Step as I poked at him with my foot.

As Step spoke, the kid flung his hair out of his eyes and peered intently at us. He saw we were awake and was on us in a flash. The three of us wrestled about madly. We could do nothing with the kid. He pinned us down with an arm around each of our necks. We made faces at him and desperate attempts to rise. With one finger he pushed us back, taking the game very seriously.

"¿Se rinde? ¿Se rinde?" he asked.

"We're finished, Villa. You got the best," cried Step.

"Sure, don't kill us, *bandidito;* give us a break."

He appeared to think that over. Then he held out his twiglike arms for us to look at.

"Mucho esfuerzo . . . strong like bull."

"Sure, sure; now scram, so's we can fix up this bed," said Step. He picked up the kid and set him on the floor.

"Say, wait a minute," puzzled Step, running his hands through his flaming hair. "Wasn't it just last night . . . ?"

"Guess so," I said. The sunlight beating down made what had happened at Mag's unreal.

"You seen her this morning?"

"Naw, not yet."

"Suppose she's told?"

"You woke up, didn't you? That's proof she ain't."

He looked at the sun.

"Must be near breakfast."

Suddenly I couldn't pretend any longer.

132

"We got to get out of here, Step."

"Wouldn't be polite to leave before breakfast."

"You said last night you just wanted to bring her home and pick up Hi Boy. Let's get away before things get bad."

"Bad for who?" he asked.

"For both of us . . . and the kid too."

"Thought maybe you was thinking soft about Sampson again."

"Maybe," I said. "But what's happened has happened."

"Just wanted to know who you're sticking by," he said.

"You found that out when I come in the room last night."

"Yeah."

"Then we're moving on?"

"Naw," he said. "Things look different now."

"How different?"

"Oh, I don't know. Not scary any more."

"I'm plenty scared," I told him.

"We're going to stay here another week and get our pay. Hell, why should we give somebody three weeks' work?"

The screen door slammed, and we could hear footsteps on the stoop. There was a noise of corn kernels swished in a pan; then, loud and clear, Anna's voice:

"Here, chick . . . chick . . . chick . . ."

A squawk followed the firm pat-pat of chicken feet.

Anna's voice was no different than on a dozen other mornings. By leaning up on our elbows and craning our necks, we were able to see over the railing. Underneath her sunbonnet her cheeks showed their natural flush.

"Hi," called the kid, who was standing in plain sight.

She turned her face toward him and smiled.

"Morning. . . . Breakfast in a few minutes."

After she had gone back into the kitchen Step flopped down on his back and swore.

"Damn, if that don't beat hell."

"What's the matter?" I asked him.

"After last night—why, she's cool as a 'cumber."

"Yeah, game kid," I said.

"And that's dames for you—throwing a fit one minute, fair-weather the next."

"Lucky for us, ain't it?"

"Well, yeah; but, Jeez, they ought to let a guy know which way the wind is going to blow."

I got a little sore. I was wrong to feel like that, because he always talked about serious things like they amounted to nothing. Still, I couldn't help speaking sharply:

"What's eating you? Are you mad because she ain't all cracked up?"

"Course not," he said. "But she sure is putting up a good front."

"Sure, she's putting up a good front; but maybe you don't like it, 'cause she's making it look like you didn't raise as much hell as you thought you did."

The corners of his mouth fell and his face flamed like his hair. I knew those signs, but I kept on.

"Boy, you take the cake—thinking about yourself, and that girl in more of a jam than both of us put together could stand. Maybe you think you done something to poke out your chest about?"

"Cut it," he gritted. "I know what I done, and I know that it's too late to start acting like I was sorry."

The kid came over and put a hand on each of our shoulders. He looked like he wanted to be angry too, but couldn't make up his mind whose side he wanted to be on. As though to interest us in something else, he pulled us over to the screen.

"There," he said, pointing at the barn. "I shoot many things . . . shoot things." He picked up his empty rifle and sighted down the barrel. "Pop . . . pop . . . pop . . . all dead."

"What'd you bag, kid? A mess of elephants?" asked Step.

136

"*Uno, dos, tres, cuatro, cinco, muchos.* . . . Big hunter."

"Must have killed five elephants," I said. "Boy, he is a hunter."

Grateful to the kid for putting us back on a joking relationship, I sat on the edge of the bed and began to struggle with my pants. Step held the legs out for me. He looked around at the kid who was walking one of the long cracks in the floor.

"You're a great little fellow, kid."

The kid glanced up impatiently.

"You hurry," he commanded.

"Okay," laughed Step.

I looked around for my socks. New and candy-striped they were. Step had just put on his pants and shoes and stood up to slip into his shirt. A flash of red, white and blue showed around his shoe tops.

"Take 'em off. Take 'em off."

"Aw, hell. I thought they were mine," he said.

I picked up his stiff socks from underneath the

bed. They smelled of weeks of sweat and moist, spoiled dirt. I pushed them under his nose.

"Don't tell me you didn't know the difference."

"There ain't much difference," he said. "Put mine on."

"The hell I will . . ."

I grabbed for him but he was gone through the doorway.

"If you want 'em, take 'em," he jeered.

The kid laughed loud and shrill. For him this was a complete return to our normal selves. His crowing was unforced. He had nothing to blanket under a shout and a laugh.

On bare feet I followed Step out of the house. Around and around the back yard we ran until we fell exhausted. The kid had been running too, but he wasn't a bit tired. He stood looking at us lying on the ground.

"Run some more."

"Can't run any more, kid," panted Step. "Out of wind."

"You run and we'll watch," I told him.

"Run, run," he insisted.

"Our feet just won't stand for it."

The kid flopped down and rested his chin on his fists. He hadn't had this much fun with us for a long time. I think he hated to see the moment pass.

"Le's go back inside," said Step. "You can have your old socks."

"No, you come see I shoot things," babbled the kid. "Backside of barn."

"Oh, all right, kid, lead on," said Step.

We followed him around to the rear of the barn. I expected to see a hawk or some other kind of bird that he had killed, but there was nothing.

"What 'd you kill?"

"Don't think he got anything," said Step. "He dreamed it."

The kid pointed at our feet where they almost touched a flat board covered with dirt. Step put his foot under the board and flipped it over.

"Look out. Jump," he cried, and in the same moment knocked the kid and me over against the barn.

"Snakes." They were stretched out side by side in the damp left by the board.

The kid laughed like a mad thing. He scrambled on his hands and knees toward the snakes. Step tried to grab him by the feet.

"Come back here, you fool. Those are rattlers."

"Sure, sure, rattler," cried the kid. He grabbed one up in his fist and held it limp in the sunlight.

"Why—why, they're all dead," said Step.

They were very dead. Some had no heads, while others had been shot several times along the length of their scaly bodies. Five now dangled across the kid's outstretched arm. Like wet ropes, they dangled —but even that can't hang with the limpness of a long dead snake.

"Jeez, you sure cleaned out a nest," I said.

"Shoot 'em all up . . . bam-bam-bam."

140

"It was good work," said Step, patting him on the shoulder. "But why in hell didn't you tell us what you had shot?"

"The laugh was sure on us," I said.

"Mucho miedo . . . much fear," laughed the kid, pointing at Step.

Step grabbed a handful of the kid's hair.

"Why, you little Mex bastard. What'd you mean, I was scared? Why, I ought to lynch you with one of these snakes." He took up one of the long bodies. "On second thought, I think I will."

"That's an idea," I cried. "Let's hang him with his own snakes."

The kid laughed and screamed as we held him against the side of the barn and draped one of the rattlers around his neck. Then Anna came around the corner of the building and the fun was over. The scaly body hit the ground. We loosed the kid.

"Morning," mumbled Step.

"Morning," I echoed.

"Breakfast is getting cold," she said.

At the word breakfast the kid was off like a shot. "Eat boy . . . eat boy . . ."

Step shuffled around.

"Want your socks now?" he asked me.

"Naw, I'll go barefoot. I ain't used to socks, anyway."

"Just as soon you had 'em."

"You keep them," I said.

"Ain't you scared of getting a stone bruise?"

"Never had a stone bruise."

"Boy, they're awful," he said, kicking in the dust.

Anna had been looking at us without blinking or shifting her gaze. Step glanced longingly in the direction of the house and then turned to face her.

"You say breakfast is getting cold?" he asked.

She didn't answer.

"Well, guess I'll go and get washed up," he said. Nobody said anything, so he just shuffled away.

Anna and me seemed to be all right after Step had

142

gone. I took her by the arm and we started to walk back to the house. Talk came naturally.

"How you feeling this morning?"

"All right, now," she said. "Guess you were pretty disgusted with me . . . last night."

"Only with myself," I told her.

"It wasn't your fault; you tried to steer us away from each other."

"I didn't try hard enough."

"What does he think about . . . about what happened?"

"Who, him? Oh, he don't think nothing."

"Ed."

"Yeah."

"About what you said yesterday . . . when we were sitting at the station . . ."

"What 'd I say?"

"You said one girl was the same as another to him."

"Yeah, well, maybe I didn't know what I was talking about."

"Well, it's on account of what you said that I have to know what he thinks about last night."

"It don't matter what he thinks, does it? Ain't you through with him for good, after what he did?"

"Belle said last night that some girls have a lot of trouble the first time. I guess it wasn't his fault 'cause I was so dumb."

"Look here," I said, "you ain't figuring on having any more truck with that guy? Leaving your old man out of it for a second, think about yourself."

"Guess I am thinking about myself. . . . I got to hold him here now. I got to be in love with him after what happened."

We were almost to the house, and I didn't know any more to say. She went on into the kitchen while I stopped to dip my hands in the dirty water that Step had failed to throw out of the washbasin. Through the screen came Sampson's deep voice saying grace. I stood until he had finished. Then I went into the kitchen in time to hear him tell Step:

"And after you sent Hi Boy home yesterday afternoon he got out his rifle and cleaned out that nest of snakes under the back porch. Got 'em, every last one."

"Won't be afraid to walk out there in bare feet any more," said Step.

I looked at Anna as she bent over to take the flapjacks out of the oven where they had been warming.

"I heard that snakes under the porch were your luck," I said.

Sampson laughed.

"Never was superstitious like most of the fruit farmers out this way."

This was the first time since we had come to Yakima that we had kept to the place on Rest Day. Neither Step nor me had the heart to do anything but play at mumblety-peg and roll one smoke after the other. We had the place all to ourselves until the cool of the evening, for Anna stayed shut up in her room and Sampson took the kid on a long hike to the dunes and farther.

Sunday night was peaceful. Anna was inside washing the dinner dishes that had been left in the sink, while the rest of us sat on the back stoop and watched the rise of the moon. The night was full of stars . . . too many even to wonder about. Sometimes when only a couple of bright stars were out Step and me would lie on our backs and wonder. There was no danger of going daffy over just a couple of sparks overhead.

As Sampson began to jabber in Spanish at the kid, I nudged Step who was below me leaning against my knees. It was good to feel him there answering the pressure by a movement of his shoulders. Here was Step like he used to be. Anna was in the kitchen doing what she would do years of Sundays after we had gone from the valley. Nothing had happened to

146

Sampson . . . nothing would happen. Because I felt like that and was glad of the pressure against my knees, I leaned down and slapped Step against the side of the head.

"Forgot your beer bottle that time," he said.

"Just wanted to let you know it wasn't your birthday." I jiggled my knees.

"I'm due a birthday. Ain't had one that I can remember."

"Didn't you never have a cake with candles when you were a kid?"

"Naw."

"Jeez, you missed it," I cried. "Why, my old lady used to bake me a chocolate cake big as—as that washbasin." I pointed to the overturned basin.

"I have birthday," broke in the kid. "Many time I have many goat and many sheep all cooked and *frijole* and . . ." He went on in a stream of Mexican patois.

"Take it easy. Take it easy," said Step. Then to Sampson: "What's he talking about?"

147

"He says that there would be a big fiesta on his birthday. There would be hundreds of pits over which they barbecued goats and sheep. He says that all night there would be feasting and dancing and the campfires on the hills would be like the stars there . . ."

"Stop it . . . stop it, he's dreaming," cried Step.

"Maybe," said Sampson.

"What about you, Step?" I asked. "Didn't you get nothing when you were a kid and it was your birthday?"

"Sure, I got something," he said. "I got sent to the mills."

That finished the talk about birthdays, and Step got up and walked toward the orchards.

"Guess you'd better be getting to bed, *amigo*," Sampson told the kid. "You've put in a long day."

That left just Sampson and me.

"He's a strange little fellow, that Hi Boy," remarked Sampson, getting out his pipe. "Wish I could find some way to make him keep that hand of his clean."

"Sure can make up some whoppers," I said.

"I don't know about that," said Sampson. "Kids don't lie like grown ups. They just have more imagination. I wish I could find out something about him, though. When I try to question him he won't say anything that makes sense. Can't even get him to tell me his real name."

"Don't suppose it makes much difference what his name is. He seems to like the new one we gave him."

"His name might be a clew to his folks."

"I guess he didn't like his folks much or he wouldn't have been running around by himself. Maybe they treated him mean or something."

We had to stop talking for a second while Anna pushed between us on her way to the yard. Heading straight for the orchards, she was gone among the trees before we picked up the thread of our conversation again.

Sampson was speaking to me, but his eyes had not returned from following Anna and there was a deep crease in his forehead. I wondered what he was thinking.

"I know it's not the habit of fellows on the road to ask one another too many questions," he was saying.

"Yeah," I agreed mechanically.

"And I know that if you just let a person alone, sooner or later he will tell you everything about himself that you want to know."

"Yeah."

"But have you stopped to think that the little fellow might have folks somewhere who are searching for him, wondering if he is alive, grieving maybe?"

"Yeah." I had fixed my eyes on that point in the new orchard where Anna had last been visible.

"Of course you know these Mexican families— plenty of goats and children. They might be glad

——" He touched my arm. "I don't believe you're listening to me."

"Sure, sure I am."

"Maybe I'd better talk about this tomorrow. I guess you're a little sleepy."

"No, I ain't sleepy . . . not a bit."

"Being around the place was too much for you boys. What did you do all day?"

"Nothing. Just laid around."

"When fellows your age who have worked all week just lie around when they could be in town, there's something wrong," he said.

We sat there in silence while the moon passed the peak of its shallow curve and began to slant the shadows of the trees away from us. Hoping to make him sleepy, I yawned.

"You must have had a hard day . . . tramping over the dunes," I suggested.

"Interesting day. Lots of little animals too tame to shoot; long talk with the kid."

"You can take a lot more than the kid. He's sleeping like a log. I can hear his breathing from here."

Sampson did not answer, and I sat and fidgeted until I could stand no more of it. I got up.

"Guess I'll find Step and get to bed myself," I said carelessly. I started away but his voice stopped me.

"Wait a minute, I'll go with you."

The ground under the apple trees was laced with shadow. We walked along the row to the old orchard. Once I stepped on a fallen apple. It crunched like crusty sand under my foot. Beside the chirping of the insects, that was the only sound.

"Maybe you'd better give a call," said Sampson.

"Step. Step, where are you?" I called.

Two shadows detached themselves from a greater patch of shadow among the trees on our right. Step and Anna. They must have been watching us.

"Hallo," said Step.

"Just looking for you," I said.

He looked at Sampson.

"Just walking and looking at the trees and sky and all," he said lamely.

"Much better than sitting on the stoop," said Sampson.

"What say let's all go over by the rail fence," I said with a show of enthusiasm. "Ought to be cool over there."

"Anna had better go on to the house," directed Sampson. "She hasn't looked too good all evening."

Dutifully she left us, still not saying a word. We waited until her slow heavy footfalls were out of our ears, then we went in the opposite direction, coming at last into the clear moonlight, the rail fence within reaching distance of our hands.

Sitting on the top rail, watching a rabbit hop and pause, hop and pause across the open desert, I waited for Sampson to speak. There was something to be said, I knew that; the sureness of that knowledge eased my mind. The rabbit ducked into a hole. Step broke the silence.

"Where I come from, the spring nights ain't as clear as this. There 'd be nothing but rain and more rain."

"Some rain here this time of the year," said Sampson, "but not when you need it most."

"I thought it would rain last night," I said.

"Should have been a storm, by rights," added Step, "only there wasn't no clouds."

"You mean the thunder?" said Sampson.

"What about that?" asked Step. "How could it thunder and the sky be clear far as you can see?"

"Must come from over in the next state," I guessed.

"Maybe," said Sampson, "and maybe like some say it's due to old Nisqually, the glacier at the foot of Mount Rainier. Anyway, it can be heard every now and then about this time of the year."

"Don't nobody know for sure what it is?" asked Step.

"The Indians around here have a story about it.

Leastways, they told Orlando and Orlando told me. It's a good story, and he believes it. And it's the only story that claims definitely to know what is behind that thunder."

"Let's hear it," said Step.

Sampson slid down off the fence and leaned with his back against it. He pointed with his pipestem over to the west.

"Those cascades are a lot of mountains—big mountains. We say that most of 'em are the footprints of volcanoes. According to the Indian legend, the great god who created everything walked around here and the valleys are the impressions of his heel and toe. The hollow of his instep left the mountains smoking high above the valleys."

"Jeez, what a foot that guy had," breathed Step.

"Well, this big fellow made the mistake of creating everything. He made the earth like a great checkered quilt, everything in its place as it was supposed to be. He put the tribes of animals on the earth, each in its proper place. He filled the rivers and oceans with fish, each kind of fish in its proper water. Then, as an afterthought, I guess, he made the tribes of men to hunt and fish on the land and in the water."

"What was the mistake in that?" I asked.

"Well," said Sampson, lighting his pipe again, "it seems as though when his work was all done, everything in its proper place, there was nothing else for him to do. He was in the way, I guess. Every time he would put his foot down somewhere he would muss something up. If he met a warrior and looked at him with his terrible eye, that warrior would die like he had been burned in a dry-grass fire. When he breathed, the winds would tear up the forest trees. When he cried, his tears would wash away the corn; and if he spat, the rivers would flood their banks and drown the countryside. He had made a big pattern and he was outside that pattern."

"Whyn't he stay put in one place?" said Step.

156

"That's easy to ask," said Sampson, "but he was a wanderer by nature. Being outside of patterns, he had to be a wanderer."

"So what did he finally do?"

"Just what you suggested; but he couldn't stay put of his own free will, and nobody could weave ropes strong enough to hold a god. The only answer was to squat right over there among the cascades and become a mountain—a terrible smoking mountain for ages—Rainier."

"What about the thunder?" we both asked.

"Thought you might fill that in for yourselves," he said. "That is, since you boys are, in a way of speaking, relatives of that poor god."

"How's that?"

"Oh, he's got a lot of relatives," said Sampson. "Most all of the wandering harvesters and farm hands that come by this way are his folks."

"You mean, because everywhere they go they muss everything up?" laughed Step.

157

"Not exactly that. Most likely nobody but me who spends all day alone under the trees would ever see the connection.

"You see, Orlando told me that story a long time ago . . . a long time ago. And after the war I watched the fellows come back to this same valley and try to fit themselves into the patterns they had been happy in before they went away." He paused to spit. "Some of them couldn't make the grade."

"We don't even remember the war," I told him.

"No, you fellows were hardly born then. But there are hundreds of youngsters around your age who were jolted out of their patterns by the big depression . . . they became wanderers. And now that they don't have to drift any more, they can't hold down a steady job, they can't get back into the pattern."

Flashes of the talk of men riding a reefer one rainy night flashed through my mind . . . A black face that moaned about a gal in Alabama . . . An ex-jockey who missed his dames and horses . . . A shifty-eyed man who was never going to stop moving . . . Step believing himself when he said: "I ain't going to knock around from job to job till I get to be a million years old." I thought about myself hitting the road when jobs gave out. I thought about myself following the crops in season. Step spoke now:

"Lots of fellers like us get hitched and stay put on jobs. I've seen them."

"Guess a lot of fellows from the war did too," said Sampson. "The old god stayed put after a fashion by squatting down among the cascades, but the Indians say that his tormented spirit still moans and moans, and in its misery sometimes breathes thunder."

"Gosh, so that's what we heard last night," said Step.

Sampson looked at his watch.

"Say, we'd better be getting back to the house," he said. "We hit the orchard early tomorrow."

We were almost to the house before he spoke again, carelessly: "I meant to tell you fellows why I never let Anna mix with the usual run of pickers that come along this way, but you got me to telling that old Indian legend and it clean slipped my mind."

For the next four days Sampson kept us so busy that at supper we were ready to fall across the table with weariness. For the first time in over six years the new orchard was being cultivated for subsidiary crops. The farm machinery was rented from a neighbor. There was a small gang plow and, in place of a harrow, a cultivator—both old and rusty machines pulled by a tractor. Step had the bright idea of coupling them all together to save time. However, the tractor proved too small and light to pull both machines at once through the tough root-strung earth between the long rows of apple trees, so the two operations had to be done separately. We took turns riding the gang plow, as that was the worse job. There was something about the fine silty dust, thrown in your face by the tread of the tractor, that left you limp as a dishrag.

When Hi Boy wasn't in the old orchard with Sampson, he would follow us in the dun-colored mornings, running in the fresh earth behind the plow, falling and shaking the dust out of the bandage around his hand. When he was there for us to call and whistle to, the time passed quicker; but he was never there very long, for when the real heat of the morning would drive all the damp out of the air he would run to the cool of the old orchard and sleep on the low branches of the trees.

At the end of the fourth day we had the ground torn up ready for the shoes of the cultivator to drag the lumpy earth. Step said on the morning of the fifth day, when we crawled out of bed:

"We got to be moving on soon."

"It was your idea to stay until we got paid."

"How was I to know he was going to work us like guineas?"

"Maybe that's so's to keep us away from Anna."

"Maybe. I wish now we'd gone on down to the wheat country east of here."

"Have to work there too."

"Yeah, but not as fast. They have to use mules there . . . tractors turn over on the hillsides."

"Couple of more days won't kill us," I told him.

"Hell, I'm dead already."

The kid had been watching us dress. He had been quiet all morning . . . maybe because his hand had started to swell again.

"I dead," he aped, and fell on the floor in a heap. We laughed and did not think any more of the hard day ahead.

Along about two o'clock the gasoline in the big drum began to get low. It was decided that Step should go into town for more gas while Sampson and I did a much-needed job of filing on the shoes of the cultivator. While we were hoisting the drum up on the truck, Anna came out of the house.

"Who's going in town?" she called.

"Step's running in for gas," I told her.

"Tell him to wait for me," she cried, and ran into the kitchen. In a few minutes she was back carrying her sunbonnet.

"Why do you want to go into town?" asked Sampson. "This is going to be a quick trip."

"It's a quick trip for me too. All the staples have given out."

"He can bring the stuff back without you," argued Sampson.

"Sure, I wouldn't forget nothing," promised Step.

"I'd sooner go myself. I want to go," she insisted.

Sampson frowned, but Anna did not wait for his consent. She put on her bonnet and climbed up to the driver's seat.

Hi Boy, seeing the truck ready to roll, came whooping toward us, waving the filthy remains of the bandage on his sore hand. Sampson looked at him and spoke quickly in Spanish. The kid replied in a chorus of *"Si, si's"* and climbed to the cab of the truck.

"He'd like the ride," explained Sampson.

"Want us to drop him by the doc's to get that hand looked at?" asked Step.

"I'll take him in myself next week," said Sampson. "You just hurry back with that gas."

With a "Hi boy" the truck was off, and we went to the tool shed to get the files.

Before following him to the orchard, I slipped into the house. In the kitchen pantry I saw flour, sugar, meal, salt, pepper, spices, bread—bacon, butter and lard were in the icebox. I wondered what would have happened if Sampson had thought to check on the staples.

He was already working when I got to the

orchard, sitting in the loose earth where we had left the cultivator, rasping at the rusty shoes with a file.

"Just went to get a glass of ice water," I told him.

"Maybe I should 've gone myself—for that gas," he said under his breath.

"I'd have brought you some ice water if I had thought."

"Oughtn't take them more 'n a couple of hours," he said.

"Two and a half at the outside," I figured.

He bore down on the file.

"A growing girl ought to have some womenfolk to talk to," he said.

It did not seem right to let him worry about Step and Anna when I only had to tell him we were leaving and relieve his mind.

"There's something Step told me to tell you," I blurted.

As though prepared for anything, he looked steadily at me.

"It's only that we're hitting the road after we get paid off," I said.

He was not surprised.

"I had expected you would."

"Not that we don't like it here," I explained.

"At that, you boys have stayed longer than I figured."

"We got to be moving. Maybe it's a good thing."

"Maybe it's a good thing," he agreed.

We worked in silence for a long time. Then we stopped to rest and smoke.

"Any idea where you're going?" he asked.

"Maybe east. Maybe back down the coast to hit the Southern Pacific."

"Why go back down the coast?"

"Easier pickings along the south route," I told him.

He thought for a long time before he spoke: "You boys figuring on taking the little feller?"

"Why, sure. Step wouldn't leave Hi Boy."

"I didn't want to talk about this right now," he said, "I got other things on my mind, but being as you boys won't be around much longer, I figure . . ."

I could read his face.

"If it's about the kid, we ain't going to leave him," I cried.

"That's up to you, but hear what I got to say—then you can decide one way or the other. That's fair, huh?"

"Maybe you ought to wait until Step gets back," I countered.

He went right on: "You know I been trying to pick the kid ever since he came here. Well, the other night he loosened up and told me something about himself. Not much, but enough to show that it's best for him not to be bumming around the country with you fellows."

"Maybe he was just stringing you," I said.

"I don't think so," said Sampson. "I can usually tell when he's lying."

167

"You mean using his imagination," I said, using Sampson's own words of the past Sunday. "Kids don't tell lies."

"All right," he smiled. "I don't think it was imagination when he told me about traveling up and down the line with a family of Mexicans—not his real folks, the kid said."

"Who was his real folks?" I asked.

"Either he didn't know, or just wouldn't tell. I couldn't drag it out of him."

"There wasn't nobody around when we picked him up," I told him.

"Yes, I'm getting to that," said Sampson. "It seems that this family was headed for a little town about fifty miles east of the hump. Maybe you know how Mexicans travel . . . ?"

"Yeah." Many times I had seen them—whole families with their baggage and goats riding the tops of the freight cars on some "slow drag."

"Somewhere out of Las Cruces a yardman came

along and kicked the whole bunch of them off the top of the freight car, even the goats. The goats must have hit on hard ground because he says all the animals had broken legs."

"That was a dirty thing to do," I said. "Jeez, I wonder why those snakes out that way hate Mexes like that?"

"That's another story," said Sampson. "But to get back to the kid, he said they robbed the railroad for food. I guess the family must have broken seals on some boxcars or something, to keep from starving after the goats were gone. Anyway, the kid said that an *official* came and took them to jail."

"Say, that's a three-year stretch, breaking seals," I cried.

"The little fellow was lucky to get away," said Sampson. "I don't know how he did it. They might have put him in an institution or something."

"Boy, what a kid," I cried. "Wanted by the police in New Mexico . . . a little *bandidito*."

Sampson laughed: "Probably nothing so exciting; but at that, he might not be so lucky if he went back."

"Wonder where he got that ten bucks," I pondered.

"What's that?"

"Oh, nothing," I said guiltily.

"You'll agree that it's best for him not to be running around the Southwest, won't you? Besides, he's only a kid. The road's not a good place for a man, let alone a little boy."

Idly, I picked up my file and ran it lightly over the shoes of the cultivator.

"To leave him can't be too much to ask," he continued. "You only met the little fellow a short time ago."

I couldn't say anything. It would have been impossible to express myself without getting sloppy. He had his land and his orchards. That made him into something. Step and me had each other and we had the kid, that was all. Everything else was like looking at the movies. There was Butch, a dog, but he was hit by a night flyer. Sampson would have laughed if I had told him we had to keep the kid because Butch was gone.

"Well, what do you say?" he urged.

Rusty old knives, belt buckles, bottle tops, pieces of string, broken watches, luck charms—all guys on the road had their pockets filled. They couldn't carry around orchards to hold them on the earth. . . .

All I could say was: "It don't matter how long you've known a feller . . . that don't mean nothing."

"The little fellow likes it here," he pleaded. "You talk it over with Step. There's two days yet to make up your mind."

The sun stretched at the shadows of the trees, the shoes of the cultivator were all gleaming, and the

171

truck hadn't shown up yet. Sampson stood upright and spit on his dusty hands before wiping them on his bandanna. A frown made white lines in the dust on his forehead.

Lying back in the shade of the trees, I tried to stop mulling over the things he had told me. There was no way to stop the mind, and with thoughts of the kid would come the name of the town, Las Cruces.

"Las Cruces . . . Las Cruces . . . The Crosses, huh?"

"Yeah, they should have been back before this," he said, squinting at the sun.

"I been through Las Cruces. I've been out of El Paso into Mexico. A gang of mud huts and a million priests, I bet."

"Maybe they had to wait for the tanker to come around before they could get that gas. But that's not like Mac, he always has enough gas in the pumps."

"Step and me ought've met that yardman outside of Las Cruces. He should be shot with about five hundred pieces of lead . . . and that's a hell of a load to carry, even in a sack."

"Guess they're back at last," cried Sampson. And on the tail of his words came the familiar "Hi boy."

"Didn't hear the car at all," I said. "Thinking too hard."

Halfway through the orchard we heard the kid's running feet, and a moment later he was upon us, almost knocking us down as he grabbed for our hands.

"Whoa, whoa," cried Sampson, swinging him up on one shoulder, talking rapidly in Spanish.

He had asked about the trip to town, but the kid would not answer. He struggled so that Sampson had to put him down. Then he was running ahead of us, shouting and leaping.

Burning with the story that Sampson had told me in the orchard, I hurried toward the truck. Step had a piece of hose in his hands, ready to siphon some of the gasoline from the big drum to four-

173

gallon cans. He stopped fiddling with the hose and turned toward me, but before either of us had a chance to speak, Sampson broke in:

"Where'd you leave Anna?"

"Dropped her off at the front door," said Step gruffly.

"You just about made us waste the whole day," said Sampson. "What happened, another breakdown?"

"It was the shopping . . ." began Step, but Sampson cut him off.

"All right, all right, we got to catch up. Let's get some of the gas out of this drum and get going." He grabbed up the end of the hose and drew a mighty breath through it. Spitting out a mouthful of gas, he held the flowing spout to one of the small cans.

We carried four cans of gasoline out to the tractor, slopping a trail through the orchards. Everything ready, Step started up the engine and I climbed to the iron seat of the cultivator. The dust and roar of the motor kept us from talking, except for shouts now and then when the dragging teeth caught a root and the tractor had to stop. It was hot work and sweat streaked the dried earth that caked our faces. Every time my teeth got on edge I would suck at the grime and spit a stream of black saliva to the ground rolling slowly beneath my feet. Step had the best of the spitting, for when he let go on the hot motor of the tractor there was a *sp-t-t-t-t-t-t* and a thin vapor pleasant to watch. Sampson joined us after a while, walking ahead of us, stamping down the long roots.

It was dusk when the kid came, bringing a bucket of ice water.

"Funny," he laughed at our dirt-streaked faces.

Sampson had been grim for a long time. Now he spoke kindly:

"Work's about caught up now. Let's knock off and catch up on our eating, what say?"

We didn't say anything. We climbed stiff-legged

175

to the ground and passed the pail back and forth between us, spitting out the first few mouthfuls of the cold water.

I sat on a wheelbarrow beside the pump and watched the kid climb up on a box to pour a bucket of water over Step's freckled body. Framed in the light of a lantern dulled by night creepers and flyers, the kid held the bucket over the flaming head and laughed.

"It's an hour now since we ate," I told Step. "I got to talk with you."

"Let 'er go, kid," cried Step, bracing himself. "Eeeeeeee!" He shivered as the icy pump water splashed over him. No sooner was the bucket empty than the kid hopped down and began to work the pump handle furiously, anxious to repeat the whole thing.

"Better c'mon, Ed," cried Step, plying the soap, "can't get in the bed with me 'less you do."

176

"Hurry and get through," I said.

"There's no hurry; we ain't going no place to-night. C'mon, get your duds off."

"Jeez, all evening I been saying I got to talk to you . . ."

The next bucket of water went unheeded over his naked body. He stopped rubbing himself and looked out from under his reddish brows.

"I know what's on your mind," he growled, "but it wasn't my idea this time. She wanted to."

"What the hell are you talking about?" Then it all became clear—why he had avoided being alone with me all evening. "Say, you mean you took Anna by Mag's again?"

My voice must have revealed how new that thought was. He looked at me suspiciously. Then he got very interested in the kid's pumping.

"Hurry up that water; the bugs are eating me up. Put some axle grease in it."

"*Si, si,* very quick axle grease," cried the kid, pumping faster.

"You heard what I just said," I told him.

He turned on me: "Jeez, why you all the time have to say so damn much? Are you God or some-body? I wonder why I don't just punch your head and be done with it." He started to dry himself with quick slaps of his shirt.

I got up and took the bucket away from the kid.

"Hi Boy, where'd you go . . . in town? You know, what place?"

He looked at me and then looked at Step.

"Don't know," he said. But as Step gave him a warning glance: "Shopping . . . go shopping."

"Aw, what you want to make the kid a liar for?" I said, pushing the little feller toward the house. "Run on away somewhere, kid. Go on, now."

Say-eyed, looking back over his shoulder, he went.

"Heck, I didn't take him inside," said Step.

"He knows damn well what you went there for."

"Well, what of it?" said Step. "He's old enough to go for the little gals himself. We been babying him too much, that's his trouble."

178

"I guess Sampson was right, in a way," I said. "Maybe we ought to leave the kid here."

He jerked up his head.

"Leave the kid . . . What 're you blowing off about?"

"I been trying to tell you. Sampson knows we're hitting the road after Saturday. He wants us to leave the kid with him."

"Nuts to him," said Step. "The kid goes with us."

"That's what I told him."

"So what 'd he say to that?"

I told him what Sampson had found out about the kid's past life. During the telling he sat with his mouth open; afterwards, he whistled through his teeth.

"How long we've known Hi Boy don't make no difference," he said, using the same phrase I had used to Sampson. "But, Jeez, it was lucky we got out of New Mexico in a hurry."

"Yeah, Las Cruces and everything. . . . We got

to cut the south route off our map. Can't risk the kid's being caught."

"Hell, there ain't no road dick in the United States I can't dodge." He swept his hand in a wide circle parallel to the ground. "We'll go the south route and spit in their eyes as we sail by."

I was not as sure as he was of sailing along spitting in anybody's eyes, but I did not argue the point because the other route, the north one, is known to roadmen as the hungry route.

"Now, we won't say anything to Sampson about not leaving the kid," he plotted. "We'll just pull out when the time comes, and nobody 'll have a chance to be sore."

Early the next morning, at a time when we were usually noisy and ready for any kind of horseplay, Step was quietly sitting on the side of the bed, staring at Hi Boy the way you stare at a circus freak.

180

He hung onto every word that passed the kid's lips, even to the Spanish that was Greek to him.

Not knowing what to make of it, the kid got a little self-conscious; but when the same thing kept up all day, he began to cringe from Step. After dinner he came to me while I was at the pump soaking my head before going back to the orchard.

"What wrong I do?" he asked.

"What 're you talking about, kid?"

He thought for awhile and then said in his funny English:

"Step, he don't please with me for last night, *si?*"

I wanted to tell him that Step was just staring because he was afraid of losing a little *bandidito,* but I couldn't let him know that Sampson had, so to speak, betrayed his confidence.

"He ain't mad at you," I assured him.

"He is not like for I say 'shopping' last night not like he tell me," said the kid.

"Naw, that ain't it." I put my arm across his shoulders and pulled him along with me toward the orchards. "That's all forgotten, see . . . forgotten."

"Oh, that all forgotten."

"Sure . . . sure."

"So, what is mad for?" His brow wrinkled. "Why mad?"

"That ain't mad what makes him stare like that," I said. "That's 'cause . . . 'cause he always gets like that this time of the year."

"He has sick . . . *¿enfermedad?*"

"Sickness, yeah, that's it. It's his rheumatism."

"What is rheumatum?"

"That's an ache in the bones. His bones hurt," I explained. "He has to sit still like that when his bones ache."

I could see that he was not satisfied with my explanation, so before he could ask any more questions I patted him on the head and trotted away.

"Be nice to the poor guy, aching bones are bad," I called back.

"*Si, si,* Hi Boy . . . *muy simpático.*"

Chuckling to myself, I caught up with Step who

was sweating and cursing as he stamped down a root caught in the shoes of the cultivator. He glowered at me.

"Whyn't you just take the whole evening off?" he grumbled. "I'm just a hired hand. Don't give me a thought."

"I just——"

"You just hell," he said. "Grab that wheel."

Climbing on the cultivator, I took the levers in my hands. The sun had disappeared and it was too dark to see the end of the row by the time I took my hands off the levers and climbed down.

The ice water was waiting. This time it was Anna who brought the pail. She stood watching us drink. Then she put her hand on Step's sweaty arm.

"Papa says you didn't have to work so long."

He shook off her hand and tilted the bucket for another gulp. On the back of his hand he wiped his mouth.

"Got to get this done by tomorrow night," he said.

"Why?" she asked. "You know, if you work too hard you might get so you don't like it here."

"Ed and me never lays down on a job of work," he said. "We can always go back to any farm we was ever at." He nodded at me.

"That's right," I seconded.

"You don't have to go back to any other farm," she told him. "This farm is as good as any in the country."

"Guess so," he grunted, and turning, he called to Hi Boy: "Race you to the house."

We followed slowly. She spoke haltingly.

"He . . . I mean you . . . aren't thinking about leaving any time soon, are you?"

So Sampson hadn't told her.

"Why do you ask that?" I hedged.

"I want to know," she said.

"Well, you see how it is with fellers like us. We never know when we're going to feel like moving on."

She stopped. Her little breasts jumped as the tears came, but there was no sound. Not knowing what to do, I stared at the hem of her cotton dress and then at the dark wet patches around her armpits. The smell of her in the still air was good.

"Until yesterday, I didn't know what it meant to me," she managed to say.

"You went to Mag's."

"I told you I would do anything to keep him here. I told you I would . . ." Wiping her eyes on her bonnet, she turned to me with a look that made her into a woman. There was a quick tightening around my groin, but I knew who the look was for.

"Something different happened yesterday," she said intensely. "I don't quite remember what it was. I knew that I was going to be hurt again, but I was ready." Her brows contracted and she clenched her hands until they were white, like paper. "Then, I wanted to be hurt—I can't say why. That was just before this feeling happened to me. It was like knowing everything and going everywhere all at the same time. It was like music . . . like I'd gone into the air like music."

As though to see if I understood, she glanced up to my face. She backed away. I was too confused to know exactly what I was doing. But then I remember my hand on her arm, myself insisting that she keep on telling me what it had been like.

"But that's all. . . . Then I came back . . . I came back."

At her high shrill tone, I dropped her arm and turned away in an agony of embarrassment. I felt myself sinking into the ground. I wanted to strike her. I didn't know what was the matter.

"I guess I shouldn't tell things like that," she said, "but I had to talk to somebody. I guess you think I'm no good."

In spite of myself I said the thing calculated to do the most harm:

"Step and me are leaving here for good after we get paid Saturday night."

She did not seem to understand.

"We're moving on—Step said so this morning," I told her.

"But he mustn't do that." She strained to look in my lowered face. "Why do you have to be moving on from one farm to the other? Why?"

"Go ask your old man," I said brutally. "He's been to college."

Leaving her in the orchard row, I lost myself among the trees. I spent a long time in a useless effort to figure myself out. I ended up at the pump, ducking my head in the water of the brass overflow basin.

Solemnly I promised myself never to return to the Yakima Valley . . . not if every apple tree sprouted solid gold fruit.

When I came onto the sleeping porch, Step and the kid were sitting on the big bed staring at each other. With two pillows behind his back, Step looked hot and uncomfortable, while the kid was fidgeting around as though one of his legs was asleep. They both let out a sigh of relief when they saw me.

"Where you been?" asked Step.

"Is food for you," said the kid, pointing toward the kitchen.

"Yeah, Anna put your supper in the oven," said Step.

"Ain't hungry." I walked over to the cot and stretched out. I didn't want to talk. All I wanted was to lose myself in sleep.

"What's eating you—are you sick?" asked Step.

I saw that I would have to talk to keep from being questioned.

"What's the idea of the pillows?" I countered.

He got red and made a gesture toward the kid.

"It's his idea."

The kid pulled the pillows into place.

188

"Nice for bones . . . poor bones," he chanted.

"Maybe he thinks there's something the matter with me," said Step. "I ain't been acting queer lately, that you noticed, have I?"

"The only funny thing you been doing is gaping at the kid all the time," I told him.

All he could think to say was: "Awwwwww . . ."

"Maybe if you quit gaping he'll forget about your bones," I said.

The pillows were dashed to the floor and savagely kicked. He stood up to his full height.

"There ain't a damn thing wrong with my bones, kid," he cried. "If you ever even think about bones again, I'll brain you."

"Boy, you're yourself again," I told him.

The kid looked over to me.

"The sick bones, they go away?"

"Looks thataway, kid," I said.

"If I thought you had anything to do with this . . ." Step loomed over me, threatening with his fist.

"Not me. I don't know a thing about it," I said, and crossed myself.

There was a low whistle from the yard. It was more a hiss than a whistle. Head tilted, eyes fixed on space, Step listened until it was repeated.

"Where you going?" I asked as he started for the door.

"Forgot to go to the can," he called back in a low voice. I heard him tiptoe through the kitchen and down the back step, then through the screen I watched his white shirt bobbing away in the direction of the barn.

For a long time I lay awake listening to the kid muttering in his sleep. I needed sleep myself, but all I could do was wait. Then cautious feet on the stoop told me Step was coming back. After a faint whispering in the kitchen, the hinges of the door to our sleeping porch cried a little. I shut my eyes and began to take deep regular breaths. When the bed sunk beneath a weight, I turned over and opened my eyes again.

"Oh, hallo," I drawled.

"Damn, damn, damn," he was cursing in a deep regular monotone. A sound of shoes hitting the floor.

"Things didn't go so good?" I tried to keep my voice even.

"Damn whores! Damn all of them," he said.

Trying to see his face through the darkness, I wondered what I could say to make him talk. I heard him drop his clothes on the floor, and then he slid under the sheet and settled on his side. After a while I began to think he must be asleep.

"Damn, they're all the same," he suddenly growled. "Once they get to know what a man is for they want to tie him hand and foot so's he can't never get away."

"Who you talking about?" I said, trying to lead him on. But he did not answer, and soon his breathing told me he was really sleeping.

Feeling that I had been cheated because I didn't

know every little detail of what happened, I lay
·there and could not close my eyes until I heard the
last night birds harshly crying in the morning.

It was hard to believe this was our last morning at
Four Mile Farm. Sampson and Step talked about
finishing up the work in the orchards and I listened
to the kid's chatter. Anna was silent, but she never
had much to say in the mornings. We all acted like
this was just the start of another working day.

After breakfast, when I was about to leave for the
orchards with the others, Anna motioned for me to
wait.

"I want you to give him a message for me," she
said. Her voice sounded all right. Maybe she had
gotten used to the idea of his leaving. "You will?"
she asked.

"Sure, what is it?"

"Tell him I'll be at Mag's tonight to say good-by.

I'll walk to town early and wait until he gets there
. . . so Papa won't think anything," she added.

"Why can't you tell him that yourself?"

"There's a reason."

Through the screen door I could see Sampson
stop and look back toward the house. I started out.

"To say good-by. Okay," I said. She held my arm.

"One more thing—don't tell him until you're on
the way to town."

Sampson looked as though he might return. I
opened the screen and jumped the stoop.

"Okay, anything you say." I could feel her in the
doorway watching as I joined the others.

With Sampson's help the work was finished before the call for dinner. As though the orchards belonged to him, Step looked around with pride.

"Reckon Ed and me did pretty good."

"Better than that," said Sampson.

"Didn't think we'd finish up here before sun-
down," said Step. "Got anything else needs doing?"

"You both more 'n earned your money," said Sampson. "We'll just knock off for the rest of the day. Don't want you boys to leave all worn out."

"Jeez, this morning wasn't nothing for us," I told him.

"Guess not," said Sampson. "You boys have proved I was right to ask you down here to Four Mile."

"Step always says that we ain't hoboes; we're out looking for a job of work," I said.

"Been good to have youngsters about," said Sampson. He looked in the direction of the house. "Sorta wish things were different, so I could really try and make you stick here."

All of a sudden I knew that I would miss Four Mile. We had been on other jobs longer, but there had been something beyond just a job here.

"Let's go in the old orchard," said Sampson. "Ain't near time to sit to table."

With the kid running ahead, picking white grubs

out of turned clods with his toes, we plodded ankle-deep through the soft earth toward the old orchard. I looked far away down one of the rows to where the house was hidden by the massed green. I thought about Anna and the tunes of the larks on cool mornings and the mountain towering out of the green of the farthest orchard. I thought how strange it would be to wake up on the floor of a box-car, jumping along on a rough track and my hips numb from the pounding.

Sampson was speaking to me. He had to repeat his words before I understood.

"Ed, did you talk to Step about the little fellow?"

"Yeah."

"And what did you boys decide?"

"You have to ask Step."

"I didn't . . . I mean, I ain't made up my mind yet," said Step.

We were in the old orchard. Here the trees were not set out in straight rows. Some of the horny limbs touched the ground and were as thick as the trunks from which they sprang. The kid ran up and down on the low branches and yelled so that we could hardly hear one another talk. Sampson plucked him off a dragging limb.

"You want to do me a favor?" he said.

The kid stopped struggling and listened.

"There were some hawks over the chicken yard this morning," he told the kid. "Hawks trying to get the chickens. You get your twenty-two out and——"

The kid did not wait for him to finish.

"Hawks. I shoot them. Will kill." He was on the ground and running as hard as he could go.

"I ain't seen no hawks," I said.

"Maybe you just didn't look in the right direction," said Sampson. "Why don't you go after the little fellow? Might get in a few shots yourself."

"You coming, Step?" I wanted to know.

"Step and I can take a smoke and have a little talk together," said Sampson.

"Okay," I agreed. I would sooner be away shooting hawks when Step told him we were not going to leave the kid. As I turned away, Step gave me a wry glance.

The kid and me made a lot of noise and craned our necks for the better part of an hour toward the sky before I began to suspect that we had been taken in on the hawk story. I glanced resentfully toward the orchards. It was all right to get rid of the kid by using a dodge, but I was a man and deserved more respect. Rolling a smoke and looking at the house, I wondered if Anna was in the kitchen. The noise around the chicken run had not brought her out on the back stoop. Yet she must have heard us. The kid came running.

"See any yet?" I hollered. There was still no sign of anyone near the kitchen door.

"Hawk is fly low . . . down like this," said the kid, showing me with his hands. "Maybe is in tree."

"Maybe. That's a thought, anyway."

197

"Go see?"

"You go . . . I been working . . . tired." I stretched my arms wide and gave a big yawn.

"We go sleep?"

"Me—me go sleep." I jabbed my finger into my chest. "You shoot hawks." I pointed at him.

"Okay, Jeez, *si, si* . . . *los mataré.*"

"Nuts," I laughed. "Go on, beat it."

He wandered away whistling the tune to which he usually sang his "Hi boy, hi boy, hi boy, hi." I knew damn well why I had sent the kid away, but on the path to the house I tried to make believe that I was really tired and going to the house to sleep.

The kitchen smelled of cooking and the table was laid out, but Anna was not there. I read the note on Sampson's plate: "Dinner is in the oven. Gone to the movies in town. Won't stay late. Anna." I opened the oven and there were the covered dishes and a meat pie still smoking. Absently I stuck my finger through the crust of the pie, not thinking that it would be too hot. With a quick gasp I cooled the burning finger in my mouth. The pie was good.

She had said that she would be waiting at Mag's. For no reason at all I played with the idea of not giving Step the message. It would be a good joke for her to wait and Step never know. I looked at the pie. "Jeez," I thought aloud, "I ought to have a keeper when I get to doing things without knowing I'm doing them." There was a big hole in the crust of the pie, but I fixed everything by pushing the crust around so the hole didn't amount to anything.

When Sampson and Step came from the orchard Sampson was smiling and had his arm across Step's shoulders. The kid joined them before they passed the barn, and I could tell by the movements of his hands that he was jabbering about hawks. Sampson laughed, and I wondered how he could be so happy when he must know that the kid was leaving with us after dinner. Sampson called to me before they reached the house:

"What's for dinner?"

"Eat boy," cried the kid.

"Meat pie, a big one," I said.

After the others had washed up and gone inside I caught Step by the sleeve of his shirt.

"You sure put it over . . . about the kid," I whispered.

He pulled away and scowled.

"Why the long face?" I asked.

"Don't know what you're talking about."

"Jeez, your face must reach to the middle of next week."

"C'mon, let's get through eating if we're going to hit the road tonight," he snapped.

"Okay. It's high time we told the kid we're moving," I said. "I guess there's no reason not to tell him outright now."

"No. . . . Wait until I give the word." He held me back.

"Sure . . . sure," I said, feeling my shoulders where his fingers had sunk into the flesh.

Not even Anna's absence could ruin Sampson's good temper that evening. He only said: "She should have asked me if she could go. Hard to raise girls, can't turn them loose like a boy." He patted Hi Boy on the head and filled up his plate.

We never traveled with more than we wore on our backs, so there was no packing to do. We stood on the sleeping porch and tied our bandannas around our necks. That was to keep the cinders from getting underneath our shirts.

"You got everything?" asked Step.

"You know damn well I got everything," I said, lifting my pants' legs to see if I had forgotten to put on my socks.

He felt in his pockets. "Yeah, my smoking tobacco's here, all right—plug's here in this pocket. Lucky tail in my coat . . . knife . . . keys . . ."

"What good are those keys without the house to go with them?" I wanted to know. He had found them in town a couple of weeks before.

He did not answer, and there was nothing for me to do but to sit and watch him fumble through all the rest of his belongings.

". . . piece of catgut . . . fish hooks . . . belt buckle . . . two dimes . . . snake rattles . . ."

I looked on in silence and with disgust. Then I began to whistle through my teeth.

"You just gotta whistle?"

"Looks like we're going to be here till morning. I got to do something with my spare time."

Outside there were all the regular night noises. They would have had to suddenly stop and start again for us to hear them. However, we both caught the new sound instantly. I strained my head listening for the faint rumble to repeat itself. It came again, even more faint.

"Sounds like thunder on the mountain again," whispered Step.

"Yeah."

"Ain't heard it for a long time."

"Aw stuff, I'm tired of sitting around waiting," I said. "Whatever's on your chest, get it off and let's pick up the kid and hustle."

"That's it," he said. "We ain't taking the kid."

"What . . . ?"

"He's staying."

"Staying . . . ?"

"Yeah, I felt funny about telling you. I'm glad it's out of the bag."

"But I thought you . . . you . . ."

"Aw hell, you shouldn'ta left me there with Sampson. But he's right, we ain't doing the kid no good dragging him around and making a bum outta him. He'll get just like us—never have no place to stop in for long. It ain't no life for a kid. Anyway, his hand's gone bad again. That'll call for a doc. An' he likes it here. He and Sampson are—aw, you know what I mean."

I knew what he meant, but maybe I had counted on Step being too thick to know what was the right thing.

"Okay . . . okay," I shouted. "What's holding us up? Let's get on out of here."

The kid stood at the gate with us while Sampson counted out our wages into Step's hand. He seemed to know that this was not going to be just another Saturday night in town. Hooking a finger in both our belts he held on, and we didn't know what to say to him. We couldn't say good-by because he was not supposed to know that we were going away.

"Sure you don't want me to run you in?" asked Sampson.

"We'd sooner walk," I told him.

Standing there at the gate got embarrassing after a while . . . the kid holding onto our belts and looking wide-eyed up at us. Sampson must have seen how hard it was going to be to leave the kid.

"I'll be driving into town in about an hour to get Anna," he said. "If you want to take the little fellow as far as the station, I can pick him up there."

"Okay," said Step. "So long."

"So long," I said.

"So long. Tell Anna so long," called Step.

Sampson gave a half salute with a limp hand, and although we did not look back I knew that he stood there until we were lost in a shoulder of the road.

The evening dusk was almost like night and the moon was below the dunes, yet the desert glowed with enough light of its own to show itself through a veil. It was a long time before we felt like seeing or talking. Holding the kid's hand, we plodded along busy with our own insides. The kid had been looking from one to the other of us, not daring to break the silence, but, perhaps, wondering. Step might have been feeling like I was—so unreal that the leg muscles had no part in putting one foot before the other. I was gliding. If you had jabbed me with a knife I would not have bled. I'd have given off air . . . folded up like a paper bag.

We were almost in town, had passed the scattered

shacks with the yellow lamps in the small windows. Step started to speak but his voice was all off key, like he had forgotten how to talk. He shut up, and we walked on until the highway turned into Main Street.

"Let's cut off Main Street. Don't want to run into Anna leaving the show."

"She's waiting for you over at Mag's," I said. "Told me to tell you."

He stopped dead and cursed.

"Sonofabitch, last night was supposed to be the last time we'd see each other. We met behind the barn. She tried to make me say I wouldn't leave. Now she wants to try again."

"Maybe she just wants to say good-by."

"I ain't got no good-bys to say," he grumbled.

We entered the lighted part of the town and instead of going to the right where the freight yards were, Step turned off to his left.

"This ain't the way."

"Don't you think I know it?" he snapped.

"You going to Mag's?"

"Yeah."

"I'd of thought you didn't want to see her from how you talk."

"Sampson 'll be in town pretty soon," was all he said.

I started to run.

"C'mon, we got to get her away from there."

"Jeez," cried Step, "you sure do catch on quick." He and the kid trotted after me.

To get to Mag's we had to pass by the pool hall and the Chinese eating joints on First Street. The street was always crowded on Saturday nights, but now it was packed with excited men—some in tight groups, others running from place to place undecided just where to light. We were too intent on our own business to stop and find out what it was all about. It got to be like a game, dragging the kid through the crowd without losing him.

207

"If we get separated, I'll see you at Mag's," called Step. He was already far ahead of me. I was held back by the weight of the kid.

"Okay, go ahead." I pulled the kid off the sidewalk. We made better time in the street. The kid was puffing like a little boiler whistle at noontime and dragged on my hand more and more. Jeez, I thought, the whole town must be here on First Street. Step was already out of sight. I picked Hi Boy up in my arms and pushed on. Mag's place was only a half block farther now. A man with lather on one side of his face and a barber's towel around his neck jostled me. I looked at him and had to laugh. Like an echo the kid's laugh followed shrilly. His voice broke suddenly and he was quiet again. I hauled him around in front of me and looked into his face. His eyes were big and a little of the white showed around the pupils. I wondered why he had laughed.

"Ain't scared, huh, kid?"

He shook his head and looked from side to side.
Throwing him back across my shoulder I went on.
The crowd thickened. More people were piling onto
First Street from across the tracks. The moon had
come up and with the street lamps made everything
brighter than a cloudy day. The thought that Mag's
house was just down the street was a disturbing
canker in my mind.

"Must be an election," I called above the voices
of the crowd, more to still my growing fear than
anything else.

Something scraped the side of my cheek. A man,
whose stringy browned arms and hairy chest bulged
out of a dirty undershirt, had stuck his stubbled
chin into the side of my face.

"Election, hell. More 'n likely a hanging," he
bawled, and was off somewhere in the crowd.

The shock of having the patchy beard against my
face, more than the words, brought me to a stand-
still. I put the kid down and looked at the people

around me. A few phrases I heard began to make sense:

"Shot . . . choked to death."

"Thrown out in the street buck naked."

"Who was she?"

"Who was her folks?"

"Ought to have cleaned this town up years ago."

"Sheriff's in there now."

"Can't catch the bastard standing around in there."

"He'll get clean away."

"Jail won't hold the sonofabitch."

"Town needs a coupla hangings."

Forgetting all about the kid who was clinging to one of my legs, I grabbed a man by the arm. I had to shake the arm violently to make him notice the grip.

"What's happened? What's happened?"

The man turned a burning face in my direction and shouted something. I repeated my question but

he pulled away. I tried to follow him. The trouble
just had to be at Mag's place. The thought was like
ice all up and down my body. I forced myself to
believe that, no matter what the trouble was, Anna
would have had sense enough to clear out. She was
probably on her way to Four Mile now. Uselessly, I
snatched at coats of people around me. Nobody
would take the trouble to tell me what had happened. At last I called to a group of boys and girls
who were skipping about like they were on a picnic.
One of the littlest of the girls answered:

"Colored man shot a woman's head off."

"What woman?"

"It rolled down the steps and into the street,"
she cried. "I saw it."

"Bunk," I said. But I could feel the spirit of the
crowd. Maybe Cooper had killed Mag. It was all
I could do to keep myself from running from place
to place telling people that I had seen Mag's head
bounce against the curbing; that it had hit my feet

and I thought it was a football. There was a glorious feeling of being strong as God Almighty in the very air . . . of having a thousand hands and feet. I laughed crazily and tried to push my way to the steps of Mag's house, but the kid was riding my leg. His upturned face was full of fear.

"We'll take it easy, kid," I said, trying to make my voice calm. He relaxed his grip, and we stayed where we were until the front door of the house opened. I held my breath. Men poured out onto the moonlit porch. A dull light reflected on leather and metal at their hips. The sheriff and another man followed with Mag between them.

All my attention was focused on the doorway. Then I breathed a sigh of relief. Nobody else was going to come out. Anna was home by now.

In one hand the sheriff held the shining four-barreled shotgun that I had seen on my first day in Yakima. The sheriff held the weapon high in the bluish-white night.

"Listen. Listen, everybody." There was silence and waiting, except for the cries of the playing children. "The man got away." There was a rumble from the crowd. "But we'll have him before morning."

Somebody shouted: "Leave it to us, we'll get him." A long yell of assent followed.

The sheriff shook the gun for silence. "Just remember that we got law in this town. There ain't going to be no lynching." He said something to his men, and they gathered around Mag in a tight body and marched to the street. The kid and I were pushed around by the trailing crowd that followed the little group toward the jail. As they passed, I got a glimpse of Mag under the street lamp. Her face was almost entirely hidden by streaked matted hair. Something had snapped, leaving her brittle; all the spring had gone out of her body. It was frightening. The kid made his little whimpering noises.

We were just about the only people left standing

in front of the house. A few latecomers were hurrying around the corner after the crowd. With half a mind to follow them, I reached down for the kid's hand. With a cry, he jerked away and ran toward the shadows by the side of the house. Coming out of the darkness was Step. He grabbed up the kid.

Step and me met under the street lamp, and before I could get out the first word, he gave a push that sent me staggering along the street in the direction from which we had come.

"The freight yards," he cried. "We got to get out of here quick."

Something that I must have known all along flashed into my mind as a certainty: Anna was not safely on her way home.

With the kid under one arm, he was off at a clip that made me hustle to keep up. I tried to question him as we ran:

"What's happened? What's happened?"

"Hurry," he gasped.

214

"But what about the kid?"

"Got to take him with us. . . . Don't talk; step on it."

We ran. Because I did not know exactly what we were running from, I filled up with panic and outdistanced him. It was not far to the yards . . . only a few blocks . . . near the center of town. The yelling from around the jail became louder as I mounted a cinder bank to the right-of-way. Carrying the kid, Step sunk deep into the loose cinders. He began to slide. I reached down a hand.

"Put the kid down. Let him walk."

Step did not listen; he grabbed for my hand.

With all my strength I tried to hold him steady and keep my own balance. I heard the cinders give. Balanced on one foot, he had no chance to save himself.

"Turn loose, we're going."

I held on.

A sharp cry from the kid and all three of us

tumbled in a mess of arms and legs down the black slope. There was no pain, but I knew that my face was skinned. It would give me hell later. Step was all right, but the kid had opened the old wounds in his palm. The moonlight was not strong enough to show just how bad the damage was, so we just stopped long enough to wind my bandanna around the hand.

"Now keep your fist balled up," I told him.

We tried the cinder bank again.

There was a "drag" on the right-of-way, and the "goat" that had just cut out a few cars was chugging in a cloud of steam on a siding. The cut cars were still rolling down a blind track where the switch engine had butted them. The road engine, with blasts of the whistle, called in the flagmen and the switchmen and then tested her air.

"Which way is this thing headed?" asked Step.

"Seattle," I guessed.

"You're crazy. She's headed east."

"Looks west to me."

We had lost all sense of direction. Maybe it was
the fall that had gotten us muddled. From the
tracks the town was plain enough, but in the night
light it looked like some place I had never seen before. Step was the one who made all the decisions,
so I waited for him to say what we would do.

"We'll look for a brakeman," he said.

But there was no time to find a brakeman. The
"highball" sounded. The kid and me looked ques-
tioningly at Step.

"Grab her."

The third car from the caboose had a black hole
in its gray side. We tossed the kid through the door
and scrambled aboard. The engine puffed furiously.
A rattling started down the line as each car in turn
took up its slack. Step slid the metal door shut.

"So long, Yakima," he whispered.

"*Adios,* Sampson," whispered the kid.

"There's somebody at the other end of the car," said Step.

"How you know?"

"Heard him hock and spit."

I tried to focus my eyes for the length of the car, but there was no distance in the black around us. Holding my breath, I listened above the hollow roar in the shaking boxcar; one noise was like another.

"More 'n likely a 'bo," I guessed.

"More 'n likely."

The kid was between us. He might have been asleep, I don't know. Over his head we put our faces together and talked softly in each other's ears.

"What happened to her?"

"She got hurt. They took her to the doc's."

"Cooper killed her? She's dead?"

"No, she ain't dead."

"You sure?"

"Shot in the arm. It was an accident."

"People said it was a colored man."

"It was Mag. She didn't mean to do it."

"But they're after Cooper."

"Mag shot at him. Anna was running for the door. Mag ain't such a good shot."

"You sure she wasn't hurt bad?"

"Bone in the arm wasn't even split. Got it from one of the deputies at the back door."

"What started the shooting?"

"I can't understand it. . . . It ain't reasonable."

"What?"

"It's crazy. They said that he was trying to rape Anna."

"Jeez, Cooper? Who said so?"

"The deputy. Said that's why Mag tried to get him."

"Maybe the sonofabitch did try."

"No. It ain't reasonable. He should try to rape her in the front room and Mag is in the kitchen?"

"Maybe he was off his nut."

"Maybe. He must have known Mag would come a-running."

"How did it get all over town?"

"Anna ran out in the street. Some men took her to the doc's. She babbled out everything."

"Guess Sampson knows by now."

"Yeah."

"Maybe she didn't tell about us."

"He'd know anyway."

"Yeah," I agreed. "I bet he's looking for us right now."

"He'll look for Cooper first. I'd hate to be in his shoes if he gets caught."

"Me too."

We kept on talking—I don't know how long. Then I opened my eyes and found that I was slumped across the kid. Sitting up guiltily, I waited for Step to say the next word. There was no word. Feeling across I found that he was slumped in the corner of the car. When had we gone to sleep? There was no time in the blackness around us. Maybe just a second, maybe hours, had passed since the last whisper between us. I was hardly conscious of the jarring rattle of the car. . . . That, like the blackness, belonged. Leaning over I shook Step awake.

"What 'd you say?" he asked.

"Nothin', I shook you."

"What for?"

"You was asleep."

" 'Scuse me. Didn't mean to fall off while you was talking," he said.

I smiled in the darkness. If he had waked up first and shaken me, I would have said the same thing to him.

After a silence he said:

"You hear what the wheels is saying?"

I listened hard.

"Sure. . . . Clack-ah-clack, clack-ah-clack, clack-ah-clack."

"Naw. . . . Hear it: Ya-kim-a, Ya-kim-a, Ya-kim-a."

Now that he had brought it up, the wheels were saying just that: Yakima Yakima Yakima Yakima Yakima Yakima Yakima Yakima Yakima Yakima. I could not stop my mind from singing with them: "Yakima Yakima Yakima." In an effort to escape the rhythm I tried to repeat another word—the first one that came in my head. In an instant the clicking wheels had copied my thought and started endlessly: Anna Anna Anna Anna Anna Anna Anna Anna . . .

"Let's talk," I said to Step.

"Yeah, let's talk out loud," he answered.

"Got any ready-mades?"

I gave him a cigarette and lit one for myself.

"Think I'll wake the kid up," he said.

"What for?"

"He always has something to talk about that don't mean nothing."

By the glow of the cigarette I could see the blur of the kid's face. Peaceful.

222

"Aw, let him skate."

"Okay," he said. "What shall we talk about?"

The wheels answered: Anna Anna Anna Anna Anna Anna Anna Anna Anna . . .

"Step?"

"What?"

"You think we should have run out like that, leaving her holding the bag?"

"What bag?" he cried. "She got herself in that mess. She didn't have no business going to Mag's by herself."

"Guess not . . ."

"Damn right she didn't."

"Wonder what Sampson did to her?"

"Nothing. What could he do to her? It's us that would have been in hot water."

"She must be feeling like holy hell," I said.

"Goddamnit, shut up," he hollered. "You know what I always said about women. One's the same as another. They're all whores at heart."

"Yeah, you always said that."

"And it still goes. Dames have to look out for themselves."

I was silent for a long while. The time clicked away and a grayness showed around the edges of the door. My behind was beginning to hurt, but I didn't pay any attention to that. It wouldn't take more than two or three days for the old calluses to come back. Step had been quiet for so long that I thought he must be asleep. I wished that I, too, could sleep and not listen to the wheels. Suddenly he spoke, and I knew that he had been sitting wide-awake like me.

"If you think it 'll do any damn good, we'll go back and get ourselves shot up," he growled.

I listened to him in amazement. A great wave of feeling for him flooded my chest. His statement didn't require any answer, and I didn't dare to make a move that might be thought mushy. I just let my knee flop over like the movement of the train had thrown it. He would understand the contact. The train clicked on into the morning: Anna Anna Anna Anna Anna Anna Anna Anna . . .

Cooper had been in the boxcar with us all night. It was the kid who found him under a bunch of newspapers at the other end of the car. His eyes were bloodshot, his yellowish skin paled by a thin crust. Tufts of hair caked with heavy grease stood upright on his head. The kid smiled like he was glad to see him. Step and me were dumfounded. We could not say a word.

"I heard you last night," said Cooper, "but I was scared to say anything."

"How'd you get here?"

"They thought you were in the dunes," Step said.

"I hit out like I was making for the dunes," said Cooper, "then I circled back."

"They think you were after Anna," said Step.

225

"They'll fill you full of shot if they get hold of you," I said.

"Reckon I don't care much," said Cooper.

"Where you gun?" asked the kid.

"Wish I had it here," said Cooper, putting his hand near his head and making a movement with his trigger finger.

"All shot now," said the kid, trying to start a game.

"Where you going to?" asked Step.

"Don't know." He looked at us curiously. "Ain't you fellers sore on me?"

"What for?" said Step. "You was nuts to run off like this. They telling some crazy stuff about you tried to rape Anna. Now they'll believe it sure."

"Yeah, you should have told them Anna got hurt by accident," I said. "You should have told them you and Mag was fighting and that was all."

"They couldn't have give you much time if you had stayed and told the truth," said Step, "but now they'll believe that rape stuff."

The kid was trying to get the car door open to let more light in. I pulled him away and opened the door. A little sunshine slanted in. Hanging out of the doorway, I saw that the engine was running almost directly into the rising sun. I pulled in my head and called excitedly to Step.

"You were right—she's headed east. The hungry route."

Step did not turn. Except where the freckles clustered, the back of his neck was glowing. I shouted again. He was saying something to Cooper. Then Cooper was giving ground and I heard him give a scared cry:

"Wait a minute. I tell you, it wasn't on the level— it wasn't——"

Step's fist landed like rock on rock against his temple. Cooper smashed against the side of the car and slid to the floor, still trying to mumble something. With an awful deliberateness, Step leaned over and caught the limp man by the collar. Cooper doubled his legs under him, but slowly he was being dragged to the open door of the "balling" car. The kid gave a sharp cry and ran into a corner, covering his face. At Step's side, afraid to try and stop him, I called again and again:

"What 'd he do? What 'd he do? What 'd he do?"

"The sonofabitch did try to rape her," was all he answered, and never stopped the slow dragging.

Cooper was sliding along on his knees. His pleading terror-marked face turned to me.

"Please . . . please . . . I didn't mean . . . It wasn't on the level . . . listen . . ."

"Let's hear what he's got to say," I pleaded with Step. He paid no attention. I leaned down to Cooper.

"Slide out of your coat—quick."

He let the coat pass over his head and Step was almost thrown through the doorway by his own effort. Cooper darted back in the corner with the kid. Blocking Step, I tried to get in a word:

228

"Wait a minute."

"Why you trying to save the bastard?" he shouted.

"I just want to hear what he has to say. Maybe he didn't——"

"He just admitted it," cried Step. "Get out of the way."

There was no telling how much longer I could hold Step without coming to blows. I didn't want that to happen. The only way out was to stop him until he had a chance to cool off.

"I'm in this just as much as you," I told him.

"So what?"

"So I got a right to hear what happened."

"Hell, I told you."

"I got a right to hear from him if I want to."

In just the few seconds we had been talking a lot of the red left his face. I knew that he was almost under control.

"You ain't no wild man," I said, taking my hands off him. "C'mon, let's hear what happened."

229

He turned his back on me and walked to the other end of the car.

"All right . . . all right, you listen to the bastard. I heard all I need to hear."

"Thanks."

"But make it snappy," he growled. "He goes out at the first stop."

I tried to get the kid to go to the other end of the "empty" where Step stood, but the boy refused to go beyond the middle of the car. There he eyed Step with frightened glances. I knew that I would be frightened too, if I saw somebody go suddenly mad and I had no inkling of the reason.

"Th-thanks . . . feller," stuttered Cooper.

"Don't thank me yet," I told him. "What did you tell Step?"

"Don't know. . . . Can't get m' wind. . . . I can't think," he cried.

I stood over him, waiting until he got himself together.

230

"You said you tried to rape her," I accused.

He grabbed at my hand.

"No—no. As God is my witness, I didn't."

"Well, what did you say?"

"I said the trouble started when I grabbed her in the front room." He looked toward Step. "But there was a reason. I swear there was a reason."

"What reason?" I pressed.

"I can't tell you," he moaned, "but it wasn't rape. I wasn't meaning to hurt her."

"You better tell me the whole thing," I said, looking toward Step. "I ain't going to protect no raper."

"But it wasn't on the level."

"Then what the hell was the idea?" I demanded.

He looked around for a few seconds as if thinking about escaping from the speeding car. Then he looked at me.

"All right," he said wildly, "maybe I want to tell somebody. Maybe I want to tell you."

I waited.

"Got a smoke?" he asked.

I gave him a cigarette and a match. He went through a few greedy puffs and then sat gathering his thoughts.

He seemed to grow suddenly calm as he sat with his eyes turned inward. His thoughts seemed to have left no room for fear, and when he spoke it was from a great distance:

"I got to tell this like it's in my mind. I been thinking about it so long till it has got set."

Leaning back, he swallowed a mouthful of smoke. The story in his head must have meant a great deal to him—just a moment ago he had been shaking and stuttering, now his voice was even and calm:

"You know me and my old woman was together for a long time. I was a hell of a feller when I first run across her . . . had brought a bunch of fish with me from the coast. Making a lot of money taking these gals around from town to town. Used to do a little gambling on the side too. Yeah, I was

232

some feller. Best-dressed feller ever hit town . . .
top pants was so tight around the ankles that if my
feet swole up an inch the pants never would come
off without ripping. Had a high-button coat that
fastened right across the chest and reached down
almost to the knees . . . split in the back . . . pin
stripe it was. White vest and pearl-handled buttons." A drop of red had begun to form on the end
of Cooper's nose, but he paid no attention. "I was
too hot for the small towns, and she knew it first
time she saw me. It was a break for her that I had
been run out of Frisco for trying to put Chink
women on the street."

I was sitting down. Step had moved within ear-
shot, but he kept his back turned like he wasn't
listening. The kid was edging toward him. There
was a little half-smile on Cooper's face as he continued to talk about these things past:

"Yeah, it sure was a break for her that day she
saw me on the corner in front of the poolroom,

sitting back on my cane, my legs straddled. She was doing good, but everything was business to her. She didn't know what a real man was till I pushed her back off her heels. There never was but one way to do a sportin' woman. While you in the mood call her every low-down thing that comes to your mind and slap hell out of her while you're cussing. After that, nothing was too good for me. I was her man for as long as I could make it good."

Step turned around to face us.

"Can't you see he's stalling?"

"It ain't no stall," said Cooper. "I got to tell this like it comes to me."

"Go ahead," I told him.

"Mag and me was through a whole lot together," he continued. "We got so we liked each other just like regular folks. And she was proud of me too. Maybe 'cause I was the only man she ever took up with that could really hit the ball . . . and almost every time. Things was all right until last year.

234

That's when the trouble started. I guess I lived pretty hard and wasn't getting any younger. It was natural enough for a man to break down. But she's a good woman still . . . wants her man often and regular. I couldn't do nothing about it any more, and I couldn't tell her what the matter was—I got my pride. Natural enough when I ain't touched her in seven or eight months, she's suspicious that outside of business I'm taking up with some little chippy or other. So she begins to fool around with guys that ain't laying a cent on the wood. I beat her a lot when I wasn't really in the mood; that was bad.

"Things didn't come to a head as long as she was jealous, and I tried to keep her that way by looking at every pair of legs that come under my eye. About a week ago I think she begin to suspect the truth. I could feel it in the way she changed. I couldn't stand it. I got my pride. After all, I was the best sweet man this side of the Rockies in my day. With a rooster like me in her house Mag was the target of every sporting woman in the West—white, black and Mex. Yessir, Mag was proud of me. I couldn't stand her being anything else. So it come to me that there was only one thing to do—to leave. But a man like me can't just walk out like that. I got my pride to think of—I got to leave with some kind of honor. I either got to leave with another woman or get throwed out 'cause of one. You kin understand that."

"Sure . . . sure," I said.

"Well, that's where Anna come in. I ain't meaning to do her no hurt—just throw her down on the couch like I'm crazy for a woman and Mag ain't good enough for me. I wait till Mag is in the other room, so's she'll hear us and come a-running. Only things ain't worked out like I figured."

"But what else had you figured on?" I asked.

"It ain't never crossed my mind that the little gal would holler when I grabbed her," he said.

236

"Ain't no woman ever hollered before when I grabbed her." He looked puzzled.

"Then Mag come running," I prompted.

"She come, all right. I had sorta thought that she would just start cussing so's I could walk out like I was insulted or something. Instead of that, she grabbed up her shotgun when she saw what was happening. Both the little gal and me broke for the door. The little gal got it in the arm as she was going out. By the time I got out some people was rushing her off to the doc's. One of the men on the street was saying that she was hollering rape and murder, so I knew they'd be after me. That's when I hit for the dunes. Only I circled around."

"How come you didn't tell them that you wasn't meaning to rape her?" I asked.

"I got my pride," he said. "I couldn't stand for nobody to know that I wasn't even fit to make a little gal."

There was nothing else I could say.

"Anyway, Mag won't ever find out now." He looked around the car. "You fellers won't never say nothing, will you?"

"If you want to take the rap, it ain't my business to say you can't," I told him.

"You ain't sore on me no more, are you?" he asked Step.

Step did not answer.

"You won't never tell," pleaded Cooper.

"Aw, tell him you'll keep shut," I said.

"Hell, I wouldn't even say his name in an outhouse," said Step. "And he's getting out of here when this train stops, don't forget."

"Got another smoke?" said Cooper.

I reached in my pocket and gave him the pack.

We were riding the Northern Pacific. Because we had money it was not such hard going. We bought sardines and bread. It would have been

238

a hungry trip if we had had to depend on the countryside for food. However, the Bitter Root and the Rocky Mountains were just ahead of us; we traveled slower and slower. It was bad enough to cross the hump going through Arizona and New Mexico; it would be hell in Montana.

We could tell when the train was about to start climbing because they put another engine in the middle to help hoist. Step watched the preparations gloomily.

"They been cutting out the empties at every division point," he said. "I'm damned if I'll go over the hump in a gondola."

Sure enough, they were not going to leave us a car to ride in. The last empty was being shunted off into the yards as he spoke.

"The president of the line should know about this," I said.

"Why don't you write him then, smart guy?" said Step.

"Us traveling farmers should have a union—that's the trouble."

"We could make the kid here the big union boss," said Step, unable to resist my fooling.

The kid looked up at us. His hand was troubling him again, so he had been quieter than usual.

"How 'd you like to be a big union boss?" I asked him.

"What I have to do?"

"Oh, just sit around."

"Just sit down?" he asked.

"Maybe a few other little things, like stacking up extra greenbacks in the corner," added Step.

"Oh, he could use those to light his cigars," I suggested.

"You have cigar?" asked the kid.

Step produced a cigar butt and lit it for him. The kid could not do much for himself with only one hand in working order.

"*Gracias.*"

"That's okay." Step turned to me. "Say, that hand is getting worse."

"Yeah, he's got to have a doctor."

"You think he can hold out until we get to the flat country?"

"Ask him how he feels," I said.

"How's the hand treating you, kid?" asked Step. He plucked at the bandaged hand like it wasn't anything of great importance.

"All right. No hurt," smiled the kid.

"It's okay," said Step to me.

"Let me see you move the fingers, kid," I said, setting him an example with my own hand.

The little feller winced as his fingers moved just a little. I felt the palm through the bandanna and it was up twice as big as it should have been.

"You sure you feel okay?"

"*Si, estoy bien,*" he said. "Not scared."

I was worried, but I hid it.

"We ought to be in Kansas in . . . let's see . . ."

"Three more days with luck, and that's traveling day and night," said Step.

"We'll get that hand fixed then," I said. "We can't stop here; this is too close to Yakima."

"If he can only hold out until we hit the flat country, we can leave him at a doctor's while we scout around," said Step.

The train was on the line waiting for the drag over the mountains. The yardmaster, or somebody else who wore a white shirt, was making a last-minute check of the little white slips of paper that were tacked to the sides of the cars.

"Can't be choosy if we're going to make Kansas in three days," said Step. "C'mon, it's that gondola for us."

The gondola was half filled with iron plates, but we piled in on top of them.

"Going to be kinda hard riding," I said, testing the iron by sitting on it and jogging up and down.

"Wait a minute." Step was over the rim of the

car and was pulling grass and weeds from the side of
an old roadbed. He passed them to me and climbed
back up.

"That ought to keep our fannies soft."

The kid between us, we settled down on the
green mat and waited.

Unconsciously adjusting our bodies to each jar
of the springless gondola, neither asleep nor awake,
we shivered in the cold night wind that poured like
ice water over the edges of the open car. There
was a mist in the air. It left our faces damp and
made breathing difficult. I think we both were
listening for the kid to whimper, but he sat as stony
as ourselves. A cold drizzle brought both Step and
me out of our coat collars at the same time.

"What we going to do?" I shouted.

"We're going to take it and like it," he shouted
back.

It was no use trying to be cheerful. To laugh
would have been to make things worse by com-

parison. As if we had spoken to each other, we leaned over the kid to protect him from the wet.

"How long you think it 'll be before we get to the next division?" I shouted.

"Five hours, the way we're crawling. Maybe longer."

Five more hours. It was so much worse when I knew exactly how long I had to suffer. The kid seemed to be in a stupor. His forehead that rested on my hand seemed to be burning up. There was nothing I could do for him. Maybe it was better that he was only half-conscious. A vision of Sampson's warm kitchen appeared in my head. I didn't think of it as a place where I would like to be. This night was just as much a part of my life as anything else. Always between the warm kitchens from one coast to the other there was the road. And you took the road as you found it.

A train passed in the night. We did not raise our heads to look. A mile off, both of us knew the fast rattle of a passenger. Step cupped his mouth close to my ear.

"Flyer."

"Yeah," I grunted.

"That's what trains was made for . . . passengers," he said.

"And freight," I added.

"We ain't neither," he said. "Don't that strike you funny?"

"Nothing strikes me funny right now," I said, trying to shrink my back away from my soaked jacket.

"We ain't even people. We ain't nothing."

"Wish I had a slug of whisky," I said.

"If there wasn't no cars, no trains, no houses, it wouldn't make much difference to us."

"You feel all right?" I asked.

"Sure. I'm just thinking things, that's all."

"Think about a slug of whisky," I advised.

After a second he said: "I thought about a whole keg of wine, but it didn't do me no good. Just as I was about to taste it some rain blew in my mouth."

"That was gin, not rain. Some of it blew in my mouth too."

"Guess I've tasted enough rain to know the difference between it and gin."

"Aw hell, go back to thinking some more," I said.

About an hour later the rain changed to sleet. Our wet clothes were stiff with ice. My leather jacket that had been like a wet rag began to crack when I moved my arms.

"Must be on top at last," said Step.

"I feel a lot warmer," I said.

"That's bad."

"Why?"

"Pinch yourself," he commanded.

I caught my nose between my stiff fingers and squeezed. There was very little feeling. I pinched with all my might.

"Hell, my face is freezing."

"We got to do something," he said. "Can't take much more of this."

"Let's move around and get warm or cold or something."

Arising slowly, pain in every joint from the effort, I felt the full force of the sleeted wind. It almost took me off my feet. Hard as it was to keep footing on the swaying plates, I managed to step around until the blood hurt in my hands, face and feet. Beside me I could see the vague bulk that was Step. He looked like he was doing some crazy dance.

"What about the kid?" I called.

"Golly, I clean forgot that he could freeze," said Step.

He leaned over and shook the kid. The boy did not raise his head. So easily did he move under Step's hand that he might well have been dead.

"Hi Boy. Hey, wake up."

Between us we raised the limp body that wanted

to sink again. The head sagged and the feet danced to every movement of the gondola.

"What you reckon is the matter with him?" chattered Step.

The small hands were on fire. His forehead was on fire. I put my arms around his waist and where his shirt and coat had pulled away from the pants there was a naked expanse of burning flesh.

"Feel here, and here." I guided Step's hand over the boy's body.

"Jeez. Jeez. We got to do something," cried Step.

Helplessly we rubbed at the kid's hands and face, calling his name and handing his limp body back and forth between us.

"This ain't doing no good." Step loosed the kid and stumbled away over the slippery plates.

"Where you going?" I hollered wildly.

"Caboose . . ."

It would be dangerous going over the slippery tops to the caboose, but if it could be done Step would do it. The train crew was human. They would stop the train and take the kid into the stove-heated caboose.

Step was out of sight before he had gone the length of the gondola. For what seemed like hours I stood without moving, the kid under one arm. Vague thoughts stabbed my mind, then one thing came clearly: a vivid picture of Step falling . . . clutching the sleeted roofs . . . tearing his nails off in a desperate effort to get a fingerhold.

"Step! Step! Come back," I screamed crazily, my voice lost in the rattle and the noise of the sleet striking like a million gourds in a Mex band. Beaten, I sunk down, the kid in a heap beneath me. It might have been tears that made my cheeks hot.

The next thing I knew there was a hand on my shoulder. Then an impatient voice:

"Snap out of it. . . . Snap out of it."

"Step?"

"Who'd you think it was—Gabriel? C'mon, get up."

I got to my feet, still holding onto the kid.

"The caboose . . . ?"

"Couldn't get that far. Lumber car's in the way.
But there's a pig shipment a little way down.
C'mon."

It was strange that he should have been stronger
than me when all I had been doing was sitting; but
the labor of carrying the kid fell on his shoulders.

How we got there, I don't know. Starting out is
clear in my mind, but the next thing I remember is
being very warm and comfortable amongst the pigs.
Later, Step swore that he and I had climbed down
the latticed side of the car and forced the door,
and then had gone back for the kid. I had to believe him. He could not have done it alone.

The car was motionless when I awoke. Grunting,
shifting pigs were all around and over me. I pushed
one of them off my head and saw that the sun was

shining. My first thought was of the kid. I cleared a space around him and raised up his head. He was breathing easily, and his face was not as hot as it had been. There was a commotion at the other side of the car as Step got to his knees.

"Goddamnit." His head had hit the roof.

He was a strange sight with his hair full of the dung that covered the floor and his eyes smeared across his face.

"How's the kid?" he croaked.

"Looks okay."

"No houses around." We were in the top compartment and could see the hills stretching away on both sides. "Can't be a division."

"We're over the hump; that's all I care about," I said.

"Yeah, let's get the kid out of here."

There were no trainmen in sight so we crawled out, dragging the kid between us. On the ground the boy seemed to come to himself and stood up on his own feet. He stood shakily and said nothing, but we were happy because he was able to do that.

"Look," said Step, "half the train is gone."

"Knew our car felt kinda dead."

"There's one of the crew," called Step. "Thought they wouldn't leave these pigs out here alone."

A man had come out of a little green shack no bigger than an outhouse. He wore the regular trainsman overalls and carried a hooked iron poker.

"Must be a car knocker," said Step.

"Hallo," cried the man.

"Hallo," we answered.

"Didn't know nobody was on this train," said the man.

"Where's the engine?" asked Step.

"Gone on to the division. These cars go over south of here on a short line." He pointed out the place where the track was switched into the weeds.

"Hell, when does a drag come along that's going on down the line?" I asked.

"Lots going through," said the man. "Don't none stop here till tomorrow 'bout this time."

"There a town close around, or a doc?"

"Nope. Eleven miles along the highway is the closest."

"This kid is sick. We can't stay here till tomorrow," I said.

"Maybe we better get back in this pig car and go over on the short line with them," said Step.

The man looked at our steaming clothes and the mess on our faces and in our hair. Going over to the pig car, he examined the slatted door.

"You fellers ain't been riding in here?"

"Sure."

"Damn," said the man.

"Had to do it. Keep from freezing."

"Damn."

"The pigs didn't mind," I said.

The man looked at us again, this time with doubt. Coming close he sniffed at our clothes and wrinkled his nose. His voice was incredulous.

"You mean to tell me you rode over the hump in there?"

"Yeah."

"Damn."

"You ain't never heard of guys doing that?" asked Step.

"Naw, but course it ain't none of my business what you 'boes do."

"We ain't 'boes," cried Step. "We're out looking for a job of work."

"That don't cut no ice with me neither," said the man, "but if I was you fellers I'd make long tracks out of here."

"How come?"

"There'll be a dick riding that pickup engine."

"So what?" said Step.

"We was only keeping from freezing," I said.

"The kid's too sick to travel any farther," said Step.

"Well, all I say is that if it was me that had broken

254

into a car, I'd get the hell out of here. The law's all writ in books. You can't argue with books. They don't care if you was cold or hot."

Step put his arm around the kid and supported the limp head on his chest. He looked defiantly at the man.

"We ain't going to walk no eleven miles, and one dick ain't going to take us to no jail neither."

"That's up to you," said the man. "Course you don't have to walk nowhere. There's a north-to-south track crosses us not a step down the line."

I drew Step aside. "Maybe we ought to listen to this guy," I whispered. "We still ain't far enough from Yakima to risk having no trouble."

"But the kid."

"He looks better," I said. "Anyway, we couldn't get him to a doc's within a day, and in just twice that time we can be in Kansas."

Step turned back to the man. "Where's that north-to-south stop?"

"Right at the crossing. Takes on water."

On our joined hands we made the kid a seat between us and started to walk the track. "So long," we called.

"So long," called the man. "Better not stop for daisy-picking. You're due for a southbound any time."

We caught the southbound, all right, but it wasn't long before we wished we hadn't. It was a hotshot, stopping only long enough at the divisions to change crews. That would have been a good thing if the kid had not taken a turn for the worse. A day out of Montana, his arm went up like a sausage and the fever was fit to blister his forehead. If only we could have taken him off the train, everything might have been all right. As it was, the train was balling along so fast we knew there was no chance of a stop before Denver. And Denver was hours away.

With the kid's lifeless head on my knees, to ease the bumps, I watched Step in the doorway. The sun flung his shadow back across the floor and up the other door to the roof of the empty.

"We should have gotten off at Cheyenne," he kept muttering.

" 'Bout how many hours longer?" I called.

"Sun's almost down. Ought to be in Denver pretty soon."

"He ain't getting no better, seems like."

"If only I'd had sense enough to find a reefer, I could have walked the tops to the caboose."

"Ain't no use blaming yourself, it was too hot for a reefer."

"Yeah, I'm blaming myself," he cried fiercely. "Why'd he stick the fork in his hand in the first place? Whose fault was it that we couldn't leave him in Yakima and was scared to get him a doc when there was a chance? Whose fault is everything?"

257

"It was going over the hump that did it. How was you to know?"

"Aw, it was my fault," he growled. "Shut up or I'll punch you one."

The kid stirred and opened his eyes.

"Step. Quick. He's snapping out of it."

At once he was by my side and we were peering into the kid's flushed face. The face was dry and scaly but his eyes were sweated and yellow. The little black pupils had faded around the edges until they sort of merged into the yellow. I don't think he saw us.

"Hi Boy, Hi Boy," called Step. "Can you hear me?"

The little feller just stared at the top of the car. I shook him a little.

"We're going to get to a doc soon. Hang on, kid."

Suddenly the flaked eyes lighted up. The thin shoulders jerked on my knees. He seemed to be straining toward Step.

"He sees you. He sees you," I cried.

"Hi boy, hi boy, hi boy, hi." And the kid closed his eyes.

"Didn't see me," said Step.

"Guess not."

He went back to his post in the doorway. There was only the faintest suggestion of a shadow now.

"How many more hours you figger?"

"Red's going out of the sky. Can't be much longer."

"He's got to have some water."

"There ain't no water before Denver."

"His tongue is all swollen up."

"You got any sardines left?" he asked.

I felt in my breast pocket and brought out a can.

"Going to open it now?"

"Yeah," he said. "The kid can drink the oil."

"That good for him?"

"Better 'n leaving his mouth all cracked," he said. And getting out his knife, he went to work on the can. "Don't trust those openers—stuck myself on one."

Drop by drop he let the oil trickle down the kid's throat. When the little feller moved his head from side to side the drops would fall on his cheeks and shine greenish in the dusk.

"You want the fish?" asked Step.

"Naw."

He threw the can outward, scattering sardines all over the floor of the car. They shone like big green fireflies in black matted grass.

"Step."

"What?"

"You think Hi Boy's going to snap out of this?"

"What the hell you talking about, think? He's just a faker, that's all. Why, we could throw him in one end of the car and forget all about him and he'd be all right. Don't talk goddam silly. Why, that kid's as tough as whitleather."

"Yeah, I guess that's right."

"Bet your life it's right."

"About how long we got now?"

"No more sun . . . I figger just a few hours."

Darkness came, and by the light of a candle stump we watched. I was worried because the boy was so still and limp. Most sick people moaned and tossed about, then they got better. He just lay there, sometimes opening his eyes and moving his lips wordlessly. And except for my occasional "How many more hours?" Step and I had stopped talking. When the moon came up and made the inside of the car silver and black, he snuffed the candle.

"Can't see the kid's face," I cried. "What'd you do that for?"

"Don't want it to burn out."

"It's a funny feeling . . . the dark."

"Might need that candle later," he said.

"You said it was only a few hours more."

"Got to play it safe."

He sat to one side, and soon smoke made the air

comfortable and drowsy. I wanted to ask him to save me butts of the cigarette, but that would have meant leaving the kid while I smoked. Somehow I felt that my body was helping the kid to stay alive, was pouring my energy into him at the points where we touched.

The smoke-tainted air was good enough; I took deep lungfuls.

With heavy rasping gasps in my ears I jerked my head up from where it had sagged down to the kid's. My lips and nose were hot like his face. I must have been taking the breath right out of his mouth. Shot through with panic, I felt for my buddy.

"Huh?"

"The kid."

He lit the candle and put his face within an inch of the kid's. Each time the little fellow's chest rose and fell we could hear a labored sobbing from somewhere in his throat.

"What's the matter with him? What's the matter?"

262

"Shut up," ordered Step. He put his hand under the boy's shirt and felt around. For a long moment his hand was still.

"What's the matter?" I finally ventured.

"Just is beating . . ."

"Just is——"

"Barely beating."

"We got to get there," I cried. "We ought to be there."

"Shut up."

"Step, we're going in the wrong direction."

"Shut up."

"We'll never get there at all."

"Goddamnit, shut up," he shouted.

With a quick movement he had his opened knife in his hand and had split the kid's shirt sleeve from shoulder to wrist. Then in the candle flame he heated the blade until it glowed red at the point.

"Get up," he said, "where you can hold the kid's arm."

"No, Step. No, you can't do that."

"Got to," he said.

"Wait," I begged. "We'll be there pretty soon."

"If some of that pus don't come out he'll never make it."

"You might do something wrong."

"I saw the doc open up that hand. It wasn't nothing. Get around here."

I let the kid's head sink to the floor and tried to rise. From hours of sitting in one spot I had lost the use of my legs. On hands and knees I crawled around the kid to Step's side.

"What 'll I do?"

"Just hold the arm up by the candle . . . steady."

Being set for something terrible I couldn't believe that with one swift movement the cutting was over. But that was only the beginning. . . . In an instant brownish-yellow pus was all over my hands and Step was stroking the arm from the shoulder down. The smell was sickening at first; and then there was no smell, except when a gust of fresh air was forced into the doorway. At such times I prayed that my arching stomach would not heave. For what seemed hours he massaged the arm. My fingers were constantly moving to keep their hold.

When we had done all we had strength enough to do, we sat watching again, not bothering to kneel up off the filthy floor of the car.

When we rolled into the Denver yards we were watching a dead boy.

We put the kid's body under a tarpaulin on a flatcar loaded with farm tools. I read the square of paper tacked to one of the boxes:

"Freight consignment. Ferris Tool Co. Albuquerque, New Mexico."

I looked at Step. His face was like a piece of old leather. I had to say something. . . .

"Can't say we run out on him," I said. "He's going back almost to where he came from."

"Yeah . . ."

"He don't have to worry 'bout Las Cruces or nothing. . . . Safe for him in New Mexico now."

"Yeah . . ."

"At that, he went something like a *bandidito* ought to go. Gee, it didn't hurt him none."

"Yeah . . ."

"We did the best we knew how; can't say we didn't."

"Yeah . . ."

"Smokes . . . cigars . . . women . . . whisky," I said in a flash-back.

"Yeah . . ."

"What you reckon they'll do when they find him? What you reckon?"

"Yeah . . ."

I guess Step hadn't heard a thing I said. I felt like hell because I couldn't say or do anything for him.

Just before the flatcar pulled out I saw Step take something out of his pocket and throw it on the

tarpaulin. A dog tail . . . luck and a smooth ride.
. . . Then we were looking after the swaying red
and green lanterns that marked the end of the
freight to New Mexico. The floodlights on the out-
skirts of the yards winked out, leaving us in darkness.

"Where to now?" I asked.

"Maybe Kansas."

"Kansas?"

"Why not? We're out looking for a job of work."
Then as an afterthought: "Ain't we?"